Sweetgrass

By Cass Dalglish

SWEETGRASS

The original art and cover design for Sweetgrass was created
by Cletus J. Dalglish-Schommer

Copies and ordering information are available from
Lone Oak Press, Ltd.
Ray Howe
Editor & Publisher
304 11th Avenue SE, Rochester, Mn., 55904
Telephone 507-280-6557.

First Printing, May, 1992

ISBN 0-9627860-3-9

Library of Congress Catalog Card Number 92-81293

For David and Dora

"...every time I think of the crucifixion of Christ
I commit the sin of envy."

Simone Weil

Molly, Jimmy, Joe, Sandra, Gert and everyone else in this novel are fictional characters – they are not meant to represent anyone, living or dead. The events in their lives are only stories. But it is not the first time that anyone has told such stories, and it will not be the last.

Sweetgrass is told this time, however, with the hope that one day the incidents that are related in the story will happen no more.

— Cass Dalglish

PREPARATION FOR MASS

Gert pushed the heavy red door shut, locking the smell of incense inside the church. Sweet smoke. Old and comfortable. Was that what Molly was trying to surround herself with? The old? The safe? Incense had the smell of eternal safety for Gert. Molly too, she supposed. For both of them, it was a supernatural perfume. Sweet smoke, essence of grace, billowing out of a church full of people.

Not a full church here tonight, though. Only ten people, but that was enough. They trudged through snow to come to her Thursday night Eucharist. They were accepting her, after all. The Bishop hadn't been sure they would when he sent her out to Sweetgrass to be the priest. A woman. First woman priest they ever saw. And a former Catholic, too. A nun. A nun turned Anglican and priest.

They didn't seem to mind.

Nobody seemed to mind. Not even her family and friends. Typical, they said. Didn't expect Gert to be a nun in the first place. She was too bold a kid. Too sassy. Nuns didn't like her. Remember the fight she had in the ninth grade with Sister DeSales? The duel with the yardstick?

Sister DeSales started it. She used to go around the classroom, cracking her yard-long ruler. She cracked all knuckles not wrapped around yellow pencils and all hands not holding books open right. She did it all the time. And one day, she did it to Gert's friend Molly.

Molly was reading St. Thomas More—assigned for history. Sister DeSales taught math.

Reason enough. Crack. A loud wooden slap against the fingers of Gert's best friend. Tears came to Molly's eyes, but she said nothing. The nun stood over Molly until the girl dropped the *Utopia* at her feet and opened her math book. Then Sister De Sales smiled, tapped her yardstick on the floor and headed up the aisle toward Gert.

Gert never looked behind her. She stared straight ahead at the blackboard. There was no pencil in her hand. Her book was

1

closed. Gert was ready.

As the long ruler chopped through the air, Gert reached up and yanked it out of the nun's grasp. A fourteen-year-old pirate, a girl cavalier, Gert leaped out of her seat. Left hand behind her back, yardstick in her right, Gert fenced the weaponless woman across the room. In and out of aisles, around the teacher's desk, behind the pole that held both American and Vatican flags—Sister DeSales was dueled into a corner. Children cheered. And the principal, Mother Vincent, came into the classroom.

Incorrigible, Mother Vincent called Gert. She sent a letter home to Gert's father. Gert was a brassy girl, it said, and bold too. She had challenged authority, gone beyond disobedience. Defiling the classroom — engaging one of the sisters in a brawl — it was a brazen thing to do.

Typical, Gert's father had responded. Bold, yes, but for his Gertrude, everything bold was typical.

It was her friend Molly who was the gentle one. Molly was the one the sisters prayed for. They kept her after school and talked about the convent. About wearing the habit. About becoming the handmaiden of God, becoming His bride. It was Molly they wanted. Instead, they got Gert. And they weren't surprised when she left. Typical.

Gert pulled on her gloves and walked down the front steps of the church. Wind cut at her neck. She tugged her scarf up, trying to protect her face from the cold.

Should have worn her hat. Shouldn't have forgotten it again. What good did a hat do left at home? It was on the radiator by the front door. Warming. As though it needed to be warmed. It was black fur, shaped like a biretta with a purple satin lining. It made her feel like a Monsignor, just owning it. But she would have felt better wearing it now, pulling it down over her dangling silver earrings so they wouldn't ice up and freeze in the wind.

Around the back of the Church, there was a small lot. Gert's jeep was parked there, covered with snow. When she opened the door, a dusting of snow fell inside the car, leaving a thin layer on the driver's seat. She brushed it onto the floor, hopped in, and started the engine.

It was bad to leave so soon. She'd only been in Sweetgrass a month, and already she had to leave. To be in Great Falls by morning. And then, a flight to St. Paul could take until tomorrow night.

2

The window scraper was on the seat next to her. It had a long red plastic brush at one end. Gert picked it up, stepped out of the car, and swept snow off the windows. Underneath the snow there was ice. She scratched it with the pointed edge, cutting the ice before she could scrape it off. Finally, it began to melt from the heat of the defroster. By the time she reached the last window, the ice was turning to slush. Gert brushed it off and got back inside.

Earliest she could be back in Sweetgrass was Monday or Tuesday. She looked in the mirror. The wind made her hair even wilder than it was that afternoon. Sandy colored curls, all twisted and blown. A mop. Simply too much hair. She needed a trim. Maybe a new style. She could go to that shop on Grand Avenue. The one Molly liked. Stay down there, until she was sure Molly was all right, and get a decent haircut, too. Might as well stay all week if she was going to miss Sunday in Sweetgrass. Sunday was the day people wanted a priest. Who came to church on weekdays anyway? A handful. Like tonight. Because they knew she wouldn't be there on Sunday.

Gert shifted into reverse. The engine whined but the tires only crunched in the icy snow as the jeep backed up and turned toward the street. No trouble. Good car. There wouldn't be any problem driving to Great Falls. Radio said the roads were open. Jeep could get through even if they weren't. At the corner, Gert stopped and turned left. Her house was out on the south end of town. Out by the marker that said "Sweetgrass." Had to stop and pick up a few things. Suitcase. Duffel bag full of cosmetics. Hat. All packed and ready at home. At Gert's parsonage. People called her house the parsonage because Sweetgrass never had one before. Never an official one. The town had always been a mission. A once-a-month stop for priests who didn't live there. Gert's place was the closest thing to a rectory Sweetgrass ever had, even if it did look like a cabin — rough cedar outside, pine inside, stone fireplace from floor to ceiling.

Up the road on the left was the marker. "Sweetgrass," it said, carved into old, weathered wood. Henry Billingcourt claimed it was the original. The one they fooled Chief Joseph with. Henry said it happened when the chief was on the run. Thought he was safe in Canada, according to Henry. Thought, when he reached Sweetgrass, that he'd crossed the border. Chief thought he got his people out of the United States. So he set up camp there and rested. But it turned out the army had moved the marker. Thirty

3

miles. Posted it inside the border. Kept Chief Joseph from getting away. Kept him and his people captive. Kept Sweetgrass in the United States.

That was Henry's story, anyway. Henry said he ought to know. It was his people who were fooled into thinking they were safe. It was his people who were caught, Henry said. He ought to know.

There was a yellow light above the front door of the cabin. It lit up the front of the house and the short driveway and the old sign across the road. Gert turned in, drove up as far as she could, and stopped. She left the jeep running and stepped out onto the snow. It squeaked under her boots as she walked to the door. Inside, things she packed were there on the couch — where she'd left them before Mass.

Mass. Gert hadn't used that word in years. Not since she turned Episcopalian. The letter from Molly yesterday made her slip.

"Please, Gert. Come now. Come and say Mass. Please, Gert. Come on, now."

Gert thought it was a joke at first. Molly hadn't been a believer in years. Not in public. She didn't act like that. She didn't say things like that. Not any more.

Not since they were kids. When Molly used to be so hung up on religion. When Molly used to crown the Blessed Virgin's statue every May. Molly was always picked to carry the crown of flowers. To place the wreath on the statue's head. Kids said the nuns always picked the girl with the best dress and Molly had so many pretty ones.

It wasn't just her dresses, though. First place, Molly never seemed to notice her clothes. She wore what was set out for her. Like the time Gert wanted Molly to wear the pink one with the bunches of white flowers. Lilacs. Little clumps of them. Gert loved that dress. But Molly said no. Her mother had that one set for Thursday. She was supposed to wear the green one that day. And she wore it.

Gert didn't think it was Molly's dresses that made the nuns choose her to crown the virgin every year. It was something inside Molly, a kind of holiness — something pure and mystical. She seemed to be able to call out for miracles and get them. Not big ones. Nothing you couldn't call coincidence. But at the time, they seemed like miracles. The violets — that was one of them — she

4

found violets for Gert. It was the day before Mother's Day. Gert was on her way to the flower shop. But she stopped in the hardware store instead because there was a basketball in the window. All her money, spent on the ball, and there she was with nothing for her mother. It was Molly's idea to go to church. To make a visit and light a candle and pray for a bouquet. They knelt together at the altar of the Blessed Virgin and whispered "Hail Mary, full of grace ..." And on the way home they found it. A field full of violets, an open field covered with blue and purple violets — enough for a hundred bouquets. A minor miracle, yes. Coincidence, maybe. But definitely something mystical. There was something mystical about Molly's religion, but nothing public. Not any more.

Molly didn't practice religion anymore. She claimed practicing liberalism was enough. And practicing law. Molly was a lawyer. A prosecutor. Making a name for herself with this latest case. A big child abuse ring, they said. It was in the Sunday Tribune. Molly was making more arrests every day.

The letter from Molly was on top of Gert's suitcase. She opened it, shook it out, looked inside, as though there had to be more to the letter than she'd found the night before. Nothing. There was nothing more there.

She would have called Molly again if she had a phone in her house. Next week, the phone company kept saying. Next week, but they hadn't come yet. Technology wasn't much help in Sweetgrass. Last night, she'd gone back into town to call.

Molly's husband, Joe, was the one who answered.

"She's fine," he said. "She's working. Always working."

"When will she be home?"

"She works at home too," he said, "brings it all home."

Joe's voice was flat. None of the enthusiasm she used to hear when he and Molly were first married. Gert always thought Joe was a great husband. Better than Molly's first husband. Joe did dishes. And when Molly was pregnant, Joe washed his own clothes. And when the baby, Jimmy, was crawling around under the dining room table, Joe talked Molly into studying law. A regular feminist hero. Man Puts Wife Through Law School. Hooray.

Joe was a judge. And rich too, if you counted his father's money. And Joe was always saying you better count it that way. Separately. Joe was older than Molly, twenty, twenty-five years

5

older. But charming. He had always seemed so charming to Gert.

"Jimmy there?" Gert asked.

"Upstairs," is all he said.

"Must be almost a teenager," Gert said, improvising now.

"Only nine."

"Long time since I've seen him, I guess," Gert said.

"Haven't missed much, " his father answered.

Something was wrong. There was a cold edge to his father's voice. No slap-on-the-back humor like you expect with that kind of remark about your child. Joe sounded like he meant it.

"If I call back in half an hour, do you think Molly will be home?"

"Be asleep," Joe said.

The conversation made no sense. No more sense than the message she received the day before. What was going on? Gert wished she'd seen more of Molly lately. Occasional letters. A phone call or two. Used to have coffee — when they lived near each other, when they had time. Always said they'd be friends no matter what, no matter how much time went by. Good enough friends not to worry about staying in touch. But it was a year, maybe two. Gert couldn't fool herself. They had lost contact.

There was a click and someone lifted the receiver on another phone.

"Hello," said a woman's voice. It was Molly.

"Molly? It's Gert. I'm in Sweetgrass. You okay?"

There was a man's laugh. A deep laugh. Rolling and echoing. Joe's laugh. And no reason for it either. It didn't fit. Nobody told a joke. Nothing was funny. Gert asked Molly if she was all right, that's all. It didn't fit, Joe laughing.

"You're coming?" Molly asked over the laughter. "Gert, you coming?"

Joe gasped. It sounded as though he had sucked his laughter into the back of his throat. As though he had swallowed it so he could hear Molly talk to Gert. He was quiet now except for his breathing. Shallow breathing, his mouth too close to the phone. Airy breathing, almost as though he were panting. Heavy breathing. And listening.

"You're coming, aren't you, Gert?" Molly was trying to tell her to come.

"Of course. Can you get any time off work?"

"Always working," it was Joe's monotone.

6

"I have a big trial coming up." Molly sounded like she was agreeing with Joe, excusing his interruption.

"It was in the paper," Gert answered. "I get the Minneapolis Sunday, way up here. You're famous."

This time Joe's voice came on loud. "She's running a witch hunt," he shouted. Then he slammed down the receiver.

"Molly," Gert said. "What on earth is wrong with him? You okay?"

"I don't know." Molly's voice quivered.

"Can you talk?"

"No," Molly said.

"Do you need me?"

"Yes," Molly said.

"Is it Joe?" Gert asked. She'd always liked Joe, liked the idea that he helped Molly become a lawyer, liked the warm old house he bought her on the West Side. But the man was behaving oddly. Showing Gert a side she'd never seen before. The phone clicked again and Joe was back on the line. This time he sounded happy.

"Glad to have you visit, Gert. It's been too long."

What a change. Jekyl and Hyde. So quick. With other people, she'd wonder if it were drugs. But not Joe. Drugs didn't fit. Not him. Alcohol? Was he drunk? No. His speech was good. His voice was clear. He just kept changing, that's all. Weird.

"Jimmy's all grown up," he said. "Molly's working too hard. When are you coming?"

Back in control. And so charming.

"Tomorrow," Gert said, until she remembered how long it would take to travel from Sweetgrass to St. Paul. "Or Friday, I guess. Molly?" she asked.

"Oh, Gert. Thank God," Molly said.

"I'll be there by Friday, Molly, for sure."

The change in Joe's voice is what worried her. One minute cold, then he's laughing, the next he's angry and then he's sweet as can be. It had to be Joe. Something about Joe that had Molly scared. Had her begging for safety like the old days. For the comfort of a Mass. Why didn't she ask about that? Why didn't she come right out and ask Molly on the phone, what are you talking about? Why do you want a Mass? Because she couldn't, not with Joe listening.

After that conversation, Gert went out to the back hall and retrieved Sunday's newspaper. There had been a column in the

7

paper by a woman named Sandra Gens. It was all about Molly and her case. Gert lifted a pile of Sunday pages and set them down on the kitchen table. She flipped through the newspaper until she found the Metro Living Section. There it was; the column was there at the bottom of the first page. Gert read Sandra Gens again:

ST. PAUL, Minn. Who is Molly Stuart? And what's she doing to our town?

That's the kind of question I'm getting lately from readers who are trying to follow the action down at the courthouse.

Every night we see more footage on the six o'clock news, another couple — handcuffed, trying to tuck their faces down into their coats to hide from the cameras, in vain — neighbors maybe, people we thought were good parents. Arrested. Soon to be on trial. What's going on? Are they really hurting their own children? If they live on my block, are they going to hurt my kids too? Have they already?

Or are they innocent?

And either way, do they have to talk about these things on TV when I'm eating dinner?

I had ten calls like that yesterday alone. Another ten the day before. And the day before that. You, the readers, the citizens of St. Paul, want somebody to tell you just exactly what's going on. You're crying out for context.

The odd thing is that you're not calling the police, not pounding on the mayor's door, not phoning your priests and ministers, and probably not lining up for couch-time with your local psychiatrist either. You're calling me. A news-paper columnist. Why me? What do newspaper columnists know anyway?

Maybe it's the guilt and innocence question. People who write columns in the newspaper are pretty good at dishing out guilt. We might not be so good at innocence, but even if we don't always know who's right, we usually know who's wrong. And we can almost always sniff out the nature of the sin as well. We know when baseball managers put in the wrong pitcher. We know when school boards close the wrong school, when Congress passes a bad tax bill, and when too much money is spent to fix up the governor's mansion. Maybe that's why you call me.

Or maybe you call me about the Molly Stuart child abuse cases be you know me pretty well. When you open your paper every morning and read my column, you get a lot of unrequested stuff dumped on your kitchen table. Pieces of my identity to clutter up your day. Bits of who I am — forty, a little too fat when viewed from the side, and worried. You know by now that I worry about people like preschoolers who have to stay up until ten at night to grab a few minutes of "quality time" with their working parents. You know I get wound up about football players who "play hurt" during their first season — when they're only eight years old. You know I'm concerned about teenagers who can't get into college because of academic scars left by open schools (or the lack of any academic aftereffects at all).

I throw troubles like these at you every morning and I expect you to pick them up and become just as concerned as I am.

So is that why you're throwing Molly Stuart's investigation back at me?

Or is it because every columnist is a lot like Mom — a mom who tells you how to stuff leftovers from all food groups into one single post-Thanksgiving casserole? A mom who knows where you should put your car keys and your glasses so you won't lose them next time? A mom who won't let bullies ambush you on your way to the voting booth or jurors' duty room. A mom who knows who the bully is.

That's exactly what one reader asked me, "Who's the bully here anyway?"

Is it Molly Stuart — a young prosecutor who may have uncovered one of the largest child abuse rings in the country? Is she the bully dividing families, ruining lives, leveling false accusations of child sexual abuse? Incest?

Or has she tapped into the violent underculture of this society? Is she mining the depths of a sexual aggression we wish weren't so familiar?

Stuart is digging all right. She may be digging so deeply she's finding what links us all to brutal instincts we'd rather not recognize in our neighbors and in ourselves.

And who should be protected here — us, the adults who don't want to be disturbed by such nasty images during dinner? Or the children, the ones who get ambushed by bullies in what ought to be the safety of their own livingrooms and bedrooms?

Okay. You've asked me to answer some questions. You want me to explain what's going on with Molly Stuart and the child abuse cases. So that's what I'm going to try to do for the next couple of weeks. From now on, I'm on assignment and you're the boss. No more unsolicited notions rolling out of the ink in my column into your morning coffee. What you asked for is what you'll get.

I wish I had a title for this assignment. A good old fashioned name like they used to give to columnists and the columns they wrote. "Mercantile Melodrama." "Political Pugilism." I once knew a nutritionist who was allowed to write a column called "The Word, the Flesh, and the Deviled Egg..." Every day they reprinted that obnoxious title. But not anymore. Now we're all minimalists. You write about food, so your column is called "Food." People who like films write a column called "Movies." If you're really smart you write a column called "Books." I'm so unfocused I

9

don't even get a title. Just a black and white silhouette of my head and shoulders and my name — Sandra Gens.

Well, I'm going to change that. For the next few weeks my column is going to have a title — a title that reflects the assignment that you, dear readers, have given me. Back in college a generation ago I read T.S. Eliot's "Murder in the Cathedral." There's a group of women in the play, or the poem or whatever you want to call it, who find themselves waiting around outside the cathedral. They say they're standing outside the Archbishop's house in the somber November air because some premonition has "drawn their feet towards the cathedral."

Is it danger that attracts them? They say no. There is no "tribulation with which they are not familiar." Then, is it safety? Not safety either. But there they are, driven, just as you have driven me. You have forced my feet out into the somber November air. I am, like the poor women of Canterbury, "forced to bear witness."

Old fashioned, indeed. I have no choice but to be archaic. I am, with those women, the chorus — like the chorus of dancers in a Greek garden, that multitude of voices singing in unison, explaining, enlightening, paraphrasing reality. We are the congregation echoing the pastor's words — Amen, Amen.

The people joining a litany — Spare us, oh Lord, Hear us, oh Lord. The faithful echoing the chant of the choir — We praise thee, oh God.

A while back I saw a play called "The Gospel At Colonnus" at the Guthrie and I finally understood why they had a chorus, what it was supposed to do in ancient times, in Greek drama. The chorus is a full gospel choir; it's a crowd of singers explaining what's going on. If you get confused, just listen to the choir. It's a concert of voices rehashing all the repercussions and responding to all the hullabaloo.

Sort of like a columnist. Sort of like me.

Well, you asked for it. It was your idea. So here goes. I shall interpret for you as though I were notes in the margin of your newspaper. I will investigate. I will review. I will report. I will wail the undersong.

My first recitation will be tomorrow. And from then on, this column will be called "The Chorus."

Sandra Gens

Wailing the undersong. That's the phrase that stuck with Gert. This journalist had used the verb "wail." And Molly was at the eye of the song. Gert picked up her suitcase and the duffel bag. It was packed so full her hair dryer bulged on the side. She had said she would make it to Minnesota by Friday and she would. As long as the weather didn't get any worse. It was cold. But it wasn't snowing anymore. She walked to the jeep and tossed the bags onto the back seat and went back into the house again.

The small red light on the coffee pot glowed in the dark kitchen. Coffee was ready. She made it before she went into town for the Eucharist. Gert went to the kitchen, filled her thermos bottle with coffee and then remembered the wine. Sacramental wine. There was bottle on the counter. She left it there so she wouldn't forget. Gert pulled open a drawer, found a brown paper sack, put the wine and the thermos inside. On the way out, she grabbed her hat off the radiator.

About a mile down the road, she took the thermos out of the sack. She wanted some coffee. With one hand, Gert twisted the red plastic cup off the top of the thermos and set it down next to her. She propped the bottle, pressing it hard against the back of the seat. The pressure helped her unscrew the lid. It hissed like every thermos she'd ever opened. Like the one she used to take to school, filled with hot chocolate in the winter. All the kids had thermos jugs. They used to bring them for breakfast, when they ate in the classroom after Mass. On Wednesdays. Every Wednesday. And on First Fridays too. And during Advent. And Lent. And whenever they sang for a feast day. Or a funeral.

Back in the old days, Molly's letter wouldn't have seemed strange at all. If somebody was sick, you asked a priest to say a Mass. If somebody died, you sent a Mass, not flowers. If you needed a gift you'd make a spiritual bouquet and promise a Mass. Or use the cards. Remember the cards? Came in the mail like Christmas seals from the lung association. Mass cards. From Dominicans. Or Trappists. Or Franciscans. Always in the middle drawer if you needed one. Take your choice.

Why did Molly want a Mass? It wasn't hard to understand. Not if you remembered how important Masses used to be.

Gert sipped hot coffee. It wasn't so strange. It did make sense. When she and Molly were kids, the Mass was everything. Social life. Music. Theater. Played out every day for them, hundreds of them, children, kneeling together to watch. Infants, in their parents' arms on Sundays, already learning the story. And what incredible high drama it was. Better than Sophocles, better than Shakespeare. Better than anything they're producing on Broadway these days. Sacred tragedy. And what an incredible mysterious leading character — Christ the victim, the savior, the ultimate hero. Think what that must have done to them, children, witnessing religious theater, witnessing sacrifice.

They knew all the lines. Together, Molly and Gert and hundreds of others at St. Elizabeth's spent hours practicing those sacred lines.

The priest would speak, "Introibo ad altare dei."

The entire church of children would respond, "Ad Deum qui laetificat iuventutem meam."

Children recited the Mass. As though they were all altar boys. Everyone participated. From the pews. Missa Recitata.

And on special days, it was holy opera. Children singing arias in a foreign tongue. They became a chorus of saints and prophets and martyrs. The priest sang. The children sang. Gert and Molly sang. Missa Cantata. Gert used to love to sing the Requiem. It seemed the chant was made for her deep alto voice. Dies irae, dies illa. Solvet saeclum in favilla. Teste David cum Sibylla.

Gert began to sing again as she drove down the snowy highway. She was barely concentrating. Her mind was on vestments — black, deep purple, red — on gold chalices, tall candles, incense swinging on a chain, voices of hundreds of children rising beyond the beams of the vaulted ceiling. It was not on the monotonous white road ahead. It wasn't until she was almost even with the little boy that she noticed him, standing at the side of the road. He seemed to appear there, like a child in a St. Christopher story. Fitting into her daydream as though he were a character from her memory, a statue, the Infant of Prague. Right there on the shoulder. Too close. It scared her. Gert stepped on the brakes and began to slide. She pumped the brakes but still felt the jeep twisting sideways on the ice. She turned the steering wheel quickly to compensate. The jeep straightened and glided by the little boy.

"Damn," she swore at herself and the little boy as well.

In the rear view mirror, the child smiled and waved and headed across the highway, dragging a plastic sled behind him.

It was a real boy, all right, and he hadn't even been alarmed. She glanced in the mirror again and she could see him stop, in the middle of the road, to wave at her a second time. Damn. Gert swore again. He was just standing there. Like Molly was that time, the boy was just like Molly was. When they were kids. When they used to run in front of cars. Only Molly did it on purpose. So she could die and go straight to heaven.

12

"We GOTTA die before we're seven," Molly said one day. They were sitting on the curb. Pulling flowers off dandelions. Dropping them into a big red pitcher full of sugar water. They were trying to make wine.

"Die before you're seven and you go straight to heaven."

"Who said?" Gert asked.

"Everybody knows that," Molly answered.

Ten minutes later, the two girls were crouched at the side of the street, waiting for a car.

"Now. Please, Gert, come on. Now," Molly screamed and ran in front of a grey and green Buick that turned out of the alley. The car screeched. Molly dropped the pitcher of dandelion wine.

The car had stopped inches from Molly.

Gert remembered pieces of broken red carnival glass, a puddle of sugar water, soggy dandelion flowers in the street. She began to cry when the driver jumped out, yelling and swearing at the girls. It was Molly who didn't cry. Molly put her arm around Gert and walked her away.

"I didn't run out into the street," Gert had confessed.

"It's okay," Molly had answered. "It's not easy," she had said. "Maybe next time," she had whispered. "It's okay."

Then, like that little boy, Molly had smiled.

Damn. Gert shouted the word at the cold air inside the jeep. Damn. That's the way Molly Stuart was, if you went back far enough. She was the kind of person who'd write the letter Gert received the day before, who'd send for a Mass, who'd want to go straight to heaven. Molly was the kind of person who was always waiting for the next time. And the next time always came.

She never ran in front of a car again, never did that one again. But she had other schemes. She was only sixteen when she heard about four black students who wouldn't leave a lunch counter in Greensboro, North Carolina. The next summer she went down South, Molly and seventy thousand others. To sit in. To ride buses. To use drinking fountains. To be dragged off. To be beaten up. To be put in jail.

And the Peace Corps. Two years in the mountains of Peru. Didn't even have a horse. She walked. Alongside a llama. Alongside that crazy guy she married down there to try to save him from the draft and Viet Nam. Allan-What's-His-Name. She got pregnant with his baby. Pregnant so he could inform his draft

13

board that he was about to be a father. And when she started to bleed in the middle of the night, when she had the miscarriage, the guy disappeared. Allan-What's-His-Name, Molly's first husband, left her with a midwife and ran. For God's sake, she practically gave away her life for that man. And then she waited another five years to divorce him.

That was the difference between Molly and Gert. Molly believed. Molly believed in people the way she believed in God. Like a child. Like a baby drinking milk. Naively suckling at whatever breast was offered. Not seeming to mind if it was empty. She had her own nourishment — faith. A vial of faith she kept under her tongue. Faith that quenched her thirst even when she drank from a nipple that was angry and dry.

Gert told her it was foolish. Told her years ago. Told her she'd been spending too much of her life trying to be a saint or something.

"Or something even worse, maybe," Molly had answered. "But why not?"

"Why not what?"

"Help people. Why not?"

" `Cause some time you're going to get hurt," Gert said.

"I'm not worried," Molly had answered.

Gert wanted more coffee but there wasn't any. She hadn't put the lid on tight and when she slammed on the brakes the thermos fell on the floor. Now it was there in a warm puddle that would turn into a patch of ice within an hour. And the wine. Where was that? Gert could smell it. She reached for the dome light. There it was, the bag, wedged between the door and the passenger seat. Sweet red liquid dripping, staining the brown paper. So much for the wine. All she had to do now was worry about convincing some highway patrolman that she had not been drinking sacramental wine out of a broken bottle.

No worry. No worry about anything. Molly said it ten years ago when she married Joe. Going for it, she said, going for happiness. Going for happiness and wealth and prominence. Going to have what she wanted. What she alone wanted. Going to think only about herself. No more hard luck stories. No more worry. Time for her to give up worry.

"All done," Molly said.

"With what?" Gert asked.

"Trying to be a martyr," Molly had answered.

14

Molly had been doing that all her life. They all had. All the
kids at St. Elizabeth's. Everybody. Martyrs were their heroes.
Martyrs were their stars. Kids might be too young for violence at a
movie. Legion of Decency rated movies "B" — that was bad, or
"C" — condemned, that was even worse. But they were never too
young to witness tragedy and sacrifice at Mass. Never too young
to hear about little girls being bludgeoned to death by evil kings,
little boys with a chest full of arrows. Legion of Decency never
tried to keep them away from that kind of blood. Martyrs' blood.
It stained all their nursery rhymes. Saints' and prophets' blood.
And Molly had such a flair for the dramatic, she'd probably go
straight for the biggest story, the biggest role. Savior's blood.
Hero-victim-savior-blood. No one would have been able to keep
Molly away from that. In the theater of their childhood, Molly
would have wanted the best part.

"All done," Gert could hear Molly's voice say, "not going to be
a martyr anymore."

But she could also imagine another Molly, an earlier, more
familiar Molly saying, "It's okay." Walking away from the broken
pitcher of dandelion wine saying, "It's not easy." Smiling and
saying, "Maybe next time."

THE CHORUS

ST. PAUL, Minn. I have no doubt that Molly Stuart is trying her best to protect the children of St. Paul. In fact, your children and mine are not the only kids Stuart worries about, she frets about her own as well.

I saw a piece on the early news night before last that I think deserves comment. It was a simple, straightforward report about Stuart and her own boy Jimmy and how much time he's been spending at the courthouse lately.

They had tape of the big orange school bus rolling up Fourth Street and stopping in front of city hall. The nine-year-old boy got off the bus and was led by an assistant county attorney into the dark recesses of the building, only to emerge — by the miracle of both television and an elevator — into the brightly lit office his mother occupies on the fifth floor. The boy then settled into a desk next to his mother's. When the camera moved around the burlap partition, we could see the boy was working on an exercise in fourth grade English grammar. Those of us for whom grammar is important will be pleased that the boy was studying. Count me in that group.

But count me in another group too. Those who had a hard time understanding the news value of that story — if prosecutor Molly Stuart decides to let her son be her sidekick for the day, what difference does it make to me or you or anybody who watches the news? After all, this is a "courthouse family." The boy's dad works there too. Why shouldn't the son of a judge and a prosecutor frequent city hall from time to time?

Well, I promised I was going to put events surrounding Molly Stuart's child abuse cases in context, so I went down to city hall to talk to reporters who've been covering the story. I wanted to know how many of them thought there was news value to Stuart having her child dropped off at her place of employment.

I found the reporters in that room at the dark end of the corridor, the one that opens into the polished wood chambers where the city council and county board meet. I understand nobody likes working there, in the same cell with reporters from every other news operation in town, sitting through the same hearings, listening to the same speeches, yet trying to come up with exclusive stuff.

Was it the temptation — the lure of the exclusive — that led a TV crew to prattle on about

16

this idle tale for over a minute and forty seconds?

The reporters all said no. They all thought it was a good story. A scoop. And a snappy one at that.

You know why? They say this isn't the first time the boy's been dropped off by his school bus. They say it's been happening all fall. They say the meaning behind the story is obvious: either Stuart's been threatened or she's become overprotective.

Either case could be significant when you consider the role she's taken as guardian of all the city's children. On the other hand, Stuart's a "city hall brat" herself, daughter of a man who was mayor of St. Paul longer than anyone in the history of the city. Perhaps she considers the courthouse a second home.

I strolled over to the County Prosecutor's office and was immediately handed a sheet of paper bearing a statement signed by the chief prosecutor. It said no threats had been leveled at Stuart or at anyone else on his staff.

I looked around for Stuart and saw a blond boy sitting on the floor, next to her desk, studying math this time. I went back to the man in rolled-up shirt sleeves who'd handed me the statement and asked where Stuart was.

"In council chambers. It's a special meeting. You ought to be there."

"You think she's smothering the boy?" I asked.

"Why don't you write a column about the need for daycare down here?" he replied. "I thought you knew how hard it is to be a working mother."

"Why does she keep him here, instead of at home with a sitter?"

"Mothers worry. Didn't you ever worry?"

Yeah. I worried. I'm guilty of waiting around until the kids are on the bus, checking with school to see if they really arrived, hoping they'll phone when they get home, wishing they'd learn to cook but fearing they'll immolate themselves in the microwave. I know about mothers and worry.

So I was ready to go back to work and write a column saying Molly Stuart isn't doing anything we all don't do from time to time. Why do you think saloon keepers let their kids spend weekends sitting on a brass bar rail? Somewhere, deep inside, parents know their kids are better off with them.

But before I wrote, I wanted to drop in on the special council session and see why the fellow with his sleeves rolled up thought I ought to be there.

Stuart was asking the council for money, for a hotel room, "for her kids" she said. She didn't want her young witnesses going to foster homes anymore.

The homes weren't good enough, she said. A more protective environment was needed. A safe house.

Well, read the front page. You'll see the council said, "No." Witnesses aren't supposed to spend a lot of time together. Not under our system.

Stuart said she was disappointed. She said many of these children fear abduction by their abusers.

In this case, that means their parents.

So much for a column about kids being better off spending the day with Mom and Dad.

And that lead us to the big question: what is this column about after all?

It's about a vigilant woman who hovers over children, trying to protect them from harm. A mother who draws her own child close at the same time that she's pulling other parents' children from their homes.

I have no doubt that Molly Stuart is trying her best to protect all of the children of St. Paul — ours and hers. But I am concerned that she doesn't trust the rest of us anymore. None of us.

By bringing her son downtown every day she's saying she no longer trusts her own neighborhood, her own home. By trying to pull the child witnesses out of foster homes she's telling us there are no longer any families where "her kids" will be okay.

She seems to be saying the children are safe only if they're with her.

Molly Stuart has good intentions. But she must remember that she can't keep every child in town safe by plunging them into the legal equivalent of the River Styx. She'll never be able to immerse them all. Besides, we all know what happened to Achilles even though his mother held him by his heel and dipped him into those famous waters of invulnerability.

Sandra Gens

18

PROCESSIONAL

Molly hung up the phone; she pushed her chair away from the desk, stood and looked for snow, even though she knew she couldn't see any from her side of the courthouse. She couldn't see windows or the river below either, couldn't see anything except burlap-covered partitions separating one attorney's desk from another. The airline said Gert's plan was late, still on the ground in Rapid City. But it would take off soon. It would land in Minneapolis that night, despite the snow. Runways had been cleared. In Minnesota, runways were always being cleared.

Molly's hair was long and black, held up in a French twist by a tortoise shell barrette. She took out the barrette and let her hair fall to her shoulders. She pulled her blazer off the back of her chair and put it on. She was cold. She was tired. She wanted to go home. Her son wasn't answering the phone. She shouldn't have let him stay home. Should have had the bus bring him downtown again no matter what the press thought. Go ahead. Let them put it on TV. Let that peeping columnist loiter around her office looking for Jimmy. Let everybody know where he was, at least that way Molly would know where he was too.

That's all she needed this week, a self-appointed mind reader naming herself the arbiter of Molly's feelings. What did she think she was doing, that Sandra Gens, with her prediction that Molly was losing faith in the community. Does she call that journalism? What did Gens write on, a typewriter or a Ouija board?

Somebody like Gens should understand the problem; she had kids, she wrote about her kids all the time, fancied herself some sort of intellectual Erma Bombeck. She ought to know Jimmy was at that age — too old for a sitter, too young to be left alone. Molly's own mother phoned when she read the column, offered to take a cab over before the end of school, to be there when Jimmy got home.

"Don't let the press bother you, dear," she said. "Your father always said, 'As long as they spell my name right...'"

Reenie — that's what Jimmy called his grandmother — Reenie would do anything for Jimmy; she loved him.

19

"She spoils him," her husband took the phone from Molly. "You spoil my boy," he said to Reenie. "You spoil my wife too. Couple of spoiled children, that's who I've got to live with. Don't come over here today. Jimmy will be fine. No. Don't." Reenie didn't want to cause trouble with Joe.

"I'll be fine," Jimmy said after Joe hung up the phone.

"You'll be a Momma's boy all your life," his father said.

"No, I'll be fine. Mom, don't worry. I want to come home. I'll be okay."

If he was okay, where was he now? Molly stood over the phone and pushed the buttons one more time. She let it ring. Three, four, five times. Ten, eleven, twelve. She let it ring until she lost count. Still no answer. She shouldn't have let Joe goad her into leaving Jimmy alone. And now he'd left her too, without a car. Joe got angry and left her downtown without a car. He was angry at lunch. Before lunch, all week, and longer, she couldn't remember any more. He was always angry. She leaned forward over her desk and, as she gripped the burlap divider with her right hand, the whole side of her body — clothes and all — seemed to turn to rubber. So she clutched the partition with her left hand too and called to the man on the other side.

"Wallblom ..." she said, "Wallblom, can you give me a ride home?"

Wallblom was working in his shirt-sleeves. He'd rolled up the arms and opened the collar and while Molly was on the phone he was reading notes jotted on a long yellow pad. He muttered, something unintelligible, because he had a pencil gripped lengthwise between his teeth. He took the pencil out of his mouth and set it on his desk and nodded at Molly.

But she had already glanced away and was packing the stack of depositions from her desk into her briefcase. When she finished, Wallblom was standing there.

"You're looking this way too often," he said.

"How's that?" she asked.

"Sick," he said.

"It's sick stuff," she lifted her briefcase and patted it and set it back on her chair. She wasn't sure Wallblom understood how tainted these cases were. Not sure he believed everything the children were saying. Especially when they talked about the ceremonies, the gowns, the candles, the sacrifice. The little girl didn't say what kind or where or if it had already happened —

Molly knew it was going to take a while to get the child to explain it. Information came slowly from the frightened. Time was needed. And patience. But she was prepared to believe it. She believed everything the children said. And she thought Wallblom ought to believe it too. He was the other lawyer on the case, her assistant. He heard everything she heard. He saw how the kids acted. How scared they were. And as long as Molly was in charge, he did everything he was supposed to. But, if it weren't for her ordering him around, Molly wasn't sure he'd be doing it. If it weren't for her, there might not be any case at all. These kids wouldn't talk to just anyone. Say what they'd been saying. If it weren't her case, the children might not have talked at all. Everybody said that — cops, investigators, social workers — none of them could calm the children down like Molly could. Make them feel safe. Get them to explain the horrible games their parents made them play. The terrible ceremonies they were made a part of.

Molly had no doubt the kids were safest with her. That's why they needed a safe house. How could the council dismiss the idea so quickly? This wasn't a normal case. Normal procedures wouldn't work. Molly had to know every word spoken to those kids; she had to be aware of every event in their lives right now. She had to be in control.

Even Wallblom admitted it. He said those kids told Molly things they'd be afraid to whisper in their sleep. Yet Molly wasn't sure Wallblom understood how wrong it all was. How wrong and sick it all was. And how common.

She went to the rack a few feet from her desk and put on her coat. When she turned back, Wallblom was holding out the keys to his car.

"Don't need it tonight," he said. "Carol's meeting me down here for dinner anyway. Take the car."

"I'd rather not," she said.

"I don't want to drive all over town," he insisted. "Especially when I'm coming back down here anyway."

"Thanks," Molly reached for the keys. She didn't like being indebted to Wallblom. Not that much. He was staring at her.

"Something else bothering you?" he asked.

"I don't need anything more than these cases," she said and turned her back to him so he couldn't see how watery her eyes were, so he couldn't see the tears she was trying to hold deep inside. There, in the office, lines were to be kept clear. Issues were to be black and white. She didn't want Wallblom finding out about her fears. He'd been teasing her too much lately. She didn't want him to see the pale grey uncertainty she was living in with Joe.

"Shouldn't have let him sell your car," Wallblom said.

"Made sense at the time," Molly answered.

And, of course, it had. She used to have her own car when she was a law student, when she had to take Jimmy to day care and go to her clerking job. Had one when she worked for Legal Aid too. Always had her own car until a couple years ago when she took the position in the county attorney's office. And then, it didn't make sense to have her own car any more. After all, Joe was a judge. He was right there in the same courthouse as Molly; it didn't make any sense at all to park two cars downtown. Or to leave Molly's sitting at home all day. So Joe sold it. He said he invested the money for Molly — it wasn't much, a few thousand dollars — but he was turning it into more, and one day he was going to teach her everything there was to learn about building capital. Molly didn't miss having a car at first. It was only lately, since she'd been so busy with the child abuse cases. Since Joe had been leaving chambers early. Since he had been leaving without her.

"When do you need it?" Molly asked.

"Whenever," Wallblom said.

"I'm supposed to pick up a friend at the airport tonight," Molly said.

"Don't worry."

"Tomorrow?" she asked. "I can bring it back tomorrow morning, if you want."

"Call first," Wallblom said and he winked.

That's what bothered Molly about Wallblom. She left the office and walked down the hall to the elevator. How could he carry on as usual? These cases ought to be interfering more, upsetting him more, having some kind of effect on him. He wasn't taking things seriously. Not seriously enough.

The elevator shut its door and carried Molly down into the garage. It gave her a sinking feeling, deep inside her chest, something was throbbing. And it was still there when she drove out of the garage, onto the street. She still felt the elevator lurching down. Pulling her down. Deep.

How could she think what she was thinking? She had no

22

proof. How could she say what she'd said? How could she say it to Joe?

She'd been accusing him of being a child abuser. Not just today. She did it Monday, and she did it last week, and before too, when she first started the cases. When the kids told her how frightened they were, how they had to obey, how they weren't allowed to talk, how they couldn't do anything right.

They reminded Molly of home. They reminded her of Joe.

And she told Joe, that day when he made Jimmy leave the table because he said the boy was manhandling the food, touching every piece of bread, spreading his germs. Molly told Joe it was ridiculous, but he wouldn't let the boy stay. Molly told Joe he was dominating Jimmy. Browbeating him. Trying to scare him.

"I'm in charge," Joe said. "I'm his father."

Molly didn't remember how it started. She didn't know if it happened all at once or gradually. Sometimes she wasn't sure if it was happening at all. But it seemed she'd been running in circles trying to keep Joe happy, trying to keep Jimmy from irritating him, trying to stop Joe, stop the berating, stop the controlling, stop the anger. She never had a name for it before, though. She never thought it was wrong. Joe couldn't mean what he was saying. He was tired. He was overworked. He was having a hard time adjusting to her being so busy, so important, so often quoted in the news. She ignored his anger. Decided his words were empty. Dismissed his behavior in the same way.

Until she met those children. Poor children, harmed children, violated children. She never would have called it abuse, what Joe said and did, not until she met those kids and they reminded her of home.

"Your complaints are pretty trivial," Joe said.

"You're abusing the boy," Molly held her ground that time at the dinner table.

But she didn't always. Sometimes she thought Joe was right when he said she was crazy, when he said she couldn't tell the difference anymore, when he said her tolerance was gone. Because it was. Parents yelling at kids, spanking babies, slapping hands, Molly couldn't watch it anymore. In the grocery store last Saturday, she saw that mother pulling and yelling, yanking that little girl up by the arms and shaking her. Molly went over and told the woman to leave the baby alone, to stop it immediately, to write down her name and address and phone number.

"You're being abusive to that child," Molly insisted.

"You're that woman, aren't you?" the mother asked. "That prosecutor."

"You've lost it," Joe said when she told him what happened. "I think you ought to see somebody. You're over the line."

But if she was, why was everything beginning to seem so clear? Especially about Joe. Why did he know everybody, parents she arrested, defendants? Why was he saying they were innocent? Why did Molly see him walking through a department store last week with one of them, Kevin Schmitt?

Schmitt was a mailman who lived out in Roseville — the first person Molly had arrested for child abuse. That's what started it, six months ago; his daughter, one little girl who wouldn't go with him or his wife, wouldn't go with either parent when they got divorced; she wouldn't go anywhere; she just sat there in the courtroom until the judge called a recess and sent a bailiff down to Molly's office to ask Molly to talk to the child. One little girl sitting in Molly's office drinking a malt and eating a Hershey bar. She asked for a napkin to clean off her face. She didn't like it when chocolate stuck to her lips, she said, and Molly didn't blame her. They looked a funny color with chocolate on them, dark purple. And even after she wiped her mouth, the little girl's thin lips seemed faintly lavender. When she ran out of chocolate bar, the little girl sucked her fingers. Not her thumb, two or three of her fingers. She scratched her thigh. But she wouldn't say why she didn't want to go home. Molly took the girl to a foster home for the night and talked to her again the next day, but still the child gave no explanation. Molly brought in a social worker and a psychologist — nothing, nothing once again. A week later, when the little girl still wouldn't go with her parents, Molly took the child for a walk in the park. They sat at the edge of a sand pit; the child took off her shoes and socks and dripped sand slowly over her toes. When her feet were buried, she took a fistful of sand and stuffed it into her mouth. Molly tried to grab her arm, block her hand from her mouth. "Why?" Molly whispered to the child, "Please tell me why."

And then the child began to talk.

Her father and mother brought neighbors over for parties, the child said. All the while she talked, she scratched at herself; neighbors, she said, and their children too. She was silent for a moment; then she began again, scratching, whispering what Molly thought at first were obscenities, tightening her fists, her whole body, bending into the sand box, crouching until finally the child stretched back and spit clots of accusation.

And Molly found out why the child did not want to go home. She took the child back to the courthouse and called in a psychologist and a social worker. Every time the child met a new person, the process began all over again, repeating a pattern of silence, clawing at herself, more silence, more shame, until finally the words were pulled out. Eventually Molly recognized the way that little girl reacted; eventually she saw that it was the way all the children she interviewed reacted; they played a repetitive theme, and they played it over and over again in the background of every case.

Kevin Schmitt and his ex-wife were the first, and once Molly got Schmitts' little girl to talk, the rest of the cases opened up — fifteen kids so far, parents, grandparents, friends invited over for parties, and the children, children invited too, and always the same theme playing in the background, frightened children who could not talk without dancing first to the repetitive theme of silence and shame.

Schmitt was out on bail now, but why was he at the department store with Joe?

"Chance meeting with a former client," Joe said. "I met the guy by chance."

Joe's client? Back before he was a judge?

"How could you represent that kind of scum?" Molly had asked.

"You're an attorney," he said. "You're supposed to remember people have rights."

Maybe Joe was right. Maybe Molly was taking everything too seriously. All those children she interviewed. All their fears. Rituals. Degradation. Despair. All of it. She could feel it. It was condensing inside of her.

Joe said she reeked of it. Said the children's nightmares had become her own. Said everything she said was twisted. Like the times she told him he abused their son.

"You scare him!" she screamed at Joe. "You swear at him. You blame him for everything. You're hurting him, Joe. There's no difference between you and those people I'm arresting!"

Joe laughed. "Laughable," is what he called it. "Get help, Molly," he said. "Get help," is all he said. And he laughed.

Last time she brought it up, Joe went out and bought Jimmy a new pair of skates and he took Jimmy and his friends for hot fudge sundaes. And they all came back smiling. And Molly apologized for her outburst. She was sorry. She'd never seen Joe touch his son. She had to admit that.

Joe said parents did things that were trivial and parents did things that were horrible and Molly couldn't tell which was which any more. She was supposed to have instincts about that sort of thing, a growl mechanism like a watchdog, but her instincts weren't working any more. Joe said they fired when there wasn't any danger. Molly didn't feel them fire any more at all.

Maybe she did need help.

But what about that boy? That fifteen year old. His parents were arrested for forcing sex on his eight-year-old sister. He'd been out of town, living with an aunt in Chicago for two years, until Molly needed him as a witness, until Monday, when Molly brought him back.

"I know that guy," he said and pointed toward her desk.

Molly reached across her desk for the picture,"Him?"she asked. "What are you saying. You know him?"

"Who is he?" the boy asked. "He looks like somebody I used to know. Some guy with my mom and dad."

"He's my husband," Molly whispered.

That's when the boy said he must have been wrong. Said he must have made a mistake.

Molly blanched. Swallowed hard. Put the photograph back on the desk. Took the boy over in the corner to the glassed-in room where they could have privacy. Asked him about his sister, and his parents, and his memories.

The boy said he didn't have any. No memories. Never knew his parents were doing anything to his sister. They never did anything to him. Silence and denial, not unlike the way it always began, Molly could feel it, the boy's shame, his fear; she could hear him scratching at himself, although he appeared to be sitting perfectly still there at the teak wood table in the glassed-in room. Molly thought the boy must be pulling and tugging at his soul rather than at his body. But this time there were no accusations congealed in the silence. This time was the first time, in all Molly's interviews, that a child did not talk at the end of the dance.

"Never did anything to me," is all the boy would say.

But somebody must have said more because when Jimmy went

to sleep that night and Joe and Molly were alone, Joe started screaming at her.

"You're ruining families. Can't you see that?"

"What are you talking about?"

"Interfering where you don't belong..." he shouted, "bringing that Justin boy back from Chicago."

"How do you know?"

"Kevin Schmitt..." Joe said. "The boy's a neighbor kid."

"I thought that was a chance meeting," Molly said. "You accidentally run into him again?"

"His lawyer called me," Joe said. "He says you're asking pretty kinky questions."

"I can't talk about Schmitt, Joe. You know that."

Joe walked over to Molly. He stood as close to her as he could without touching. His voice was low and scratchy. He whispered, "About me..." He leaned forward and his knee bumped Molly's thigh, "About me..." he whispered again. "You're asking questions about me."

Molly stepped back. "He said he knew you, Joe," Molly said. "He pointed at your picture."

Joe went over to the mantle. There was a photograph of Molly there, in a brass frame. He picked it up and dropped it on the tile in front of the fireplace. The glass cracked. Joe put his heel on it and ground the broken glass into smaller fragments.

"If you don't stop," he said, "I'll stop you." Then he walked away.

It was very quiet in the house. Molly sat, all night, in the chair next to the fireplace, writing to Gert. She tried to explain how she felt, how frightened she was of Joe. She told her about the children, about the one that morning who talked of sacrifice. She said she sensed evil, smelled it sometimes, smelled sulphur. Her picture still lay next to the fireplace and Molly imagined it burning. She described flame curling around the face, licking at her forehead. What would he do to her? Would he arrange an accident? Would he start a fire? Is that why she was imagining flames? She was afraid to sleep. She would have to stand watch. She told Gert. She wrote it down. But when she read her vague uneasy feelings drawn out on paper, she was surprised at how insane her ideas appeared. Molly took another sheet of paper and wrote a different note to Gert, a short one. Then she put on her coat, walked to the box across the street, and mailed the second

27

letter. When she came back inside, Joe was there in the kitchen holding out his hand.

"I'm sorry," he said. "I was angry."

She stood, saying nothing. He reached over and touched her arm.

"I've done some thinking," he said. "Now I know why the boy thought he knew me."

He gave Molly a gentle tug, "TV. It's from TV and newspapers and running for office for God's sake. It's not your fault. I understand."

Joe tried to pull Molly toward him. She didn't move. He wrapped his arms around her, "I'm sorry, " he said again.

Molly began to cry. It had been a long time since he had been tender. He drew her closer to him. It felt good. Tenderness felt good. She didn't want it to go away. She allowed herself to forget what he'd done to her picture. He pressed her head, gently, against his chest. She wanted to believe him about Schmitt and the boy. She needed to believe him. And for a while, she did.

Like she wanted to believe him again now, driving Wallblom's car home in the snow. She wanted to be sure again. To believe Joe again like she had the other morning. But her doubt could flare as easily as his anger, and he'd been angry all week, angry at lunch, talking about the boy again, talking about Schmitt again, leaving her there, in the restaurant.

She tried to force her mind away from it. Back to driving. One-way streets. Molly hated them. She had to go down Wabasha, turn on Fourth, turn again on St. Peter, around the courthouse, around the hotel, around the civic center, it was the only way to Kellogg Boulevard and the bridge that separated downtown St. Paul from her house across the river. Round and round, worse yet, around in the snow. A thick clot of disappointment filled Molly's chest. She tried to take a deep breath but she couldn't. She couldn't clear it out. The chunk of heavy air was stuck, pushing hard against her ribs. Pressing against her back. Sapping her. Draining her. Making her dizzy. Like the circles. Like going around in circles. Molly was always going around in circles. Back to the children. Back to Joe.

Maybe Joe never did touch Jimmy, but he didn't have to, he had other ways, he had rules instead: practice cello, play hockey, no noise, play a solo, not out loud. Be better. Be stronger. Be in bed. Be awake. Where's Jimmy? Jimmy's never home. Jimmy's always home. Jimmy's in the shower again. Always dirty. Doesn't hear. Doesn't listen. Jimmy's a coward. Jimmy, be a man.

"It's my job as a father to make all the rules," that's what Joe had said.

And his rules made Molly run in circles. Keep them. Help Jimmy keep them. Help me. Help us both.

Molly tried again to clear the heavy chunk of air but it stayed, lodged in her chest. Windshield wipers thumped and squeaked. Otherwise it was quiet. No music. Molly didn't feel like music. Lately, all she ever felt was sorry.

Molly turned onto the bridge that stretched from bluff to bluff across the Mississippi. She didn't look down. Didn't look from side to side. She stared, hard, at the tail lights on the car in front of her. She'd thought about leaving Joe before. She'd thought about it. But she didn't, because she didn't think she had any real reason to go. It wasn't like Joe was really harming her and Jimmy, physically. Not like that at all. She was simply frightened of him. And tired. She wished she could do things so he'd be happy. She wouldn't mind being tired if it made him happy. She had a good career, she had a good home. She had it all, really. Why did she have to worry all the time? Why did she have all the fear? It could all be in her mind. Joe said it was all in her mind. Her fears weren't Joe's fault. Couldn't be his fault. Being afraid is something that's your own fault.

Molly wanted the whole thing to stop. She needed a different kind of thought. She longed for an evening full of freshness, an evening full of joy and calm. A Friday like they used to have — with wine and cheese and bread and music. A Friday that made her want to dance. When was the last time she and Joe danced?

Molly looked at her watch. Gert's plane wouldn't be in yet. She had time to stop home first, to find Jimmy and take him with her. She'd feel better if she had Jimmy with her. Molly'd always been different from other women, women who were managing careers and kids and homes like she was. They seemed happy to be away from their kids. But Molly didn't like it at all. She never liked surrendering Jimmy to babysitters and daycare centers. When she did errands, she liked having him safe beside her in the car. She enjoyed looking at him, enjoyed talking to him.

"It's like you're refusing to give birth," Joe had said. "It's strange, Molly. It's embarrassing. You drag that kid everywhere. Kids shouldn't be everywhere. Kids not only shouldn't be heard, they shouldn't be seen."

Maybe that's why he dared Jimmy to stay home alone. Maybe that's what fathers are for, to force the issues, to spur the children into adulthood. Mothers didn't do that; at least Molly didn't. Maybe Joe was just being a good father.

Or maybe he was jealous. It was hard on a father, having a son, Molly knew that, hard having to share the love of a woman with a child. She wanted to go home before the airport, to talk to Joe. She might even say she was sorry. She could do it one more time. It was her turn.

Maybe it was still possible to turn the cold night into a feast, to have fun with Gert, and Jimmy, and Joe. Forget the lunch. Forget what he said. Don't think about it. Forget he left her downtown. Some people would say he had a right to be angry, anyway, with all her accusations. Don't ask why he left. Don't think about why. Don't think about what she feared. Don't think.

After all, how did she expect him to react?

"You're going to lose a perfectly good husband, " he'd said, "if you can't regain your sanity."

Perfectly good. Molly had just as much proof that Joe was perfectly good. Why didn't she concentrate on that?

Don't abandon him. Calm him. Believe in him. Why did that boy know Joe? Because he's famous. He's a judge. His picture's in the paper. There's nothing more to say. Don't fear Joe. Don't leave. Be happy for once. Be happy. Happy with a husband. Happy with a man. Accept his tenderness. Touch his face. Trace your fingers down his neck. Rest your hands on his shoulders. Feel his heat. And your own.

Molly remembered how they used to stroke each other. She remembered touching him. Brushing her lips along his thighs, loving the taste of a gentleness she thought was Joe's alone. She loved it, when he would let her. If he would let her. Even now, if only he would let her. She would tell him how beautiful she found him — the white and grey and silver of him — soft hair curling toward the flat of his stomach. Molly would breathe and talk of love until her own passion would silence her. If only he would let her.

But he would not let her. He had his own way to love. He had games. And he wanted Molly to play.

"Play with me," he would say, "or I will go away."

And always, in the past, Molly had played.

30

"Only words," Joe would say. "Only fantasy and dreams and words."

And Molly would play. Dreams. Fantasies. Words. That's all.

"Play," he would insist.

And she would play until his dreams held her too tight. Until his fantasy crashed hard into her soul and bruised it. Until the cases. Since the cases, she couldn't play at all because his words reminded her of other words. Other games. Games the poor children were forced to play. Ceremonies. Rituals. Degradation.

"Don't you know the difference between fantasy and reality?" He would ask her. "Is this what you did to your first husband?" he would say. "Is this how you made him run away?"

And he would call her crazy. And he would go away. He would abandon her, like he did in the restaurant. Don't think. Don't ask why. Be strong. Let it make you strong. But Molly couldn't find her strength. Driving across the bridge, she wanted to cry out for help. She was bouncing in her own uncertainly; she felt buffeted, dazed. When she passed the church at the end of the bridge, she wanted to stop. There, at St. Michael's. Stop there and run inside and pull the statues from the walls and make them tell her what was going on. She wanted saints and angels on the stained glass windows to tell her. She wanted God to tell her.

"What should I do?" Molly whispered into the empty quiet of the car. "Why don't I know what I'm supposed to do?"

Molly slowed down, but she didn't stop. She drove beyond the church. At the corner, she turned left and pulled into a lot behind a small grocery store. She bought a loaf of hard-crusted Italian bread and a pound of yellow cheese and then she went two doors down to the liquor store and picked out a jug of dry red wine. A feast. Gert would be there soon and it was still possible to turn a cold night into a feast. She got back in the car and drove up the hill toward home.

31

PRAYERS AT THE FOOT OF THE ALTAR

Rapid City was not a bad place, not in Gert's opinion. At least not the airport. Gert could still smell the hot cider and mulled wine. Strange for an airport to smell that way. Like opening the door to a tea shop where they sell herbs and spices and all those tiny knick-knacks. That's one thing Rapid City did right: Kiosks selling tankards of hot drinks all winter long. Gert had three mugs of cider, sitting there, most of the afternoon, waiting for her plane. It used to be hard for her to wait, but she was beginning to learn patience. The convent hadn't taught her. Not the seminary either. It was time that was teaching her. Passing years. Years full of days, days full of hours, hours full of quiet spaces. At forty-one, she was beginning to enjoy quiet spaces whenever she found them. Nowhere to go. No one to talk to. No task to finish. No choice but to contemplate. To read. To think. To wait. Nothing else to do. No matter how concerned she was about Molly. She had to wait. And the taste and aroma of the spicy drink had made the waiting pleasant.

Now, finally, she was on her way.

She stretched her legs out into the aisle. She sighed. She drew her legs back and she buckled her seat belt. Only one hour and thirty five minutes before she was in Minnesota. The flight attendant walked by, making sure carry-on luggage was tucked away, checking belts, asking the man in front of Gert to put his seat in an upright position. Stewardess, they used to call them, back when she and Molly wished they could be one. Fly all over the world. See Europe. Be beautiful. Get paid. How great. Gert closed her eyes. She always said a prayer before a plane took off. As long as it was on the ground, taxiing along the runway, there was still time for a good, solid prayer. After it was in the air, there wouldn't be anything more she could do.

"You all right, Miss?" the attendant touched Gert's shoulder. "Everything all right?"

"Absolutely," Gert said. She was done with her prayer.

The attendant walked to the front, took a seat, and buckled herself in. The plane was already off the ground. Gert opened the

32

magazine she'd bought in Great Falls. What if they had become stewardesses? What would they be doing now? Flying from Rapid City to Minneapolis? Trying to serve sandwiches and drinks and coffee to a crowd of impatient people, make them happy, get them there safely, in less than two hours? Maybe the nuns were right.

"Not for bright girls," the nuns used to say. "That is not work for a bright girl."

Nuns had a list of things they didn't want bright girls to do. Being a stewardess was one. Typing was another. Cooking and sewing. Singing. Art. Everything practical. Everything enjoyable. What was left? Trigonometry. Physics. Latin. Greek. That's all they got. The bright girls. College prep girls. Molly and Gert.

"They never taught us to clean a house, Gert," Molly'd said at their last high school reunion. "Somewhere along the line, when all other women learned to do laundry, you and I were doing Latin instead."

Skills they weren't allowed to learn. Skills were saved for other girls. For girls who didn't do Latin.

"I think they taught them other things too," Molly told Gert at that reunion.

"Like what?"

"Like how to enjoy life. Look around the place. You can see it. They're all happy."

"You're happy," Gert said.

"Yeah?" Molly answered. "You too?"

Gert had never been happier. She had it all. Plucking priesthood from one tree and womanhood from another. Biting into both. Swallowing juices of fruits never before mixed. A new Eve. Original disobedience, maybe that was it. In order for her to follow her calling, to be a priest, she had to break some rules. Eat the fruit. Here we go again. Reach. Stretch. Fly. She wasn't supposed to be able to fly. But she could. Look.

The ground below was white. Was it the snow covered earth or the clouds? Gert couldn't tell the difference.

"Are you happy, Gert?" Now that she thought about it, Molly seemed to be hoping for a negative answer. But Gert told her she'd never been happier.

"Really?" Molly thought they were missing something vital. Some knowledge. Some wisdom. Some preternatural gift.

"Look around," she said, "at the rest of them. They know

33

something we don't. While we were doing Cicero, they were doing 'How to survive with a man.' "

Gert closed the magazine. She was displeased with herself. It should have been obvious at the high school reunion. Molly as much as told her. Molly wasn't happy. And Gert hadn't noticed. And even when the letters stopped, when Molly quit writing, when there was no communication, Gert ignored that sign too. Thought Molly was busy, that's all. Thought Molly was happy. Thought this time Molly had a perfect marriage. Thought she understood what kind of man Joe was. The kind of man Molly said he was when she fell in love with him ten years ago.

"Is this a good man?" Gert asked Molly at the time.

"Beautiful," Molly had answered. "Beautiful."

"Just?"

"Just what?"

"You know," Gert said. "You know. I mean 'just,' like honest. Pure of spirit. Free of iniquity, deceit..."

"That's a mouthful," Molly laughed.

"You really love this one?" Gert had asked.

"I'm enthralled," Molly had said.

"I remember when you married that other guy, Allan-What's-His-Name."

"You don't even remember his name. Anyway, you weren't there. That was in Peru. Don't tell me you know what I should have done in the case, because you weren't there."

"That wasn't love," Gert said.

"There were going to draft him. Right out of the Peace Corps. For an unholy war, Gert, they were going to draft him."

"That was to save the world, then, or to save Allan. But it wasn't love."

Pretty free with advice back then, Gert thought. The flight attendant put a plastic glass of Coke and a foil sack of almonds on the tray in front of Gert. Advice about nothing. Going around giving advice about a marriage that had been over for years. You have to be pretty clever to do that. Should have given better advice about Joe. Should have told her not to marry him. Not to marry somebody twenty five years older than her. A father figure. Somebody to replace her dad. Perfect dad. Molly's was close to perfect. Engineer by training. Inventor by choice. Politician by popular demand. Mayor of St. Paul in 1951. Candidate for governor. Winner of votes. Shaker of hands. Rider in parades.

Father of Molly. Mr. Mayor. He was quite the hero. But he died of a heart attack before his time. Maybe before Molly's time.

It was hard on her, his death. "Cut off at the knees," she told Gert. Molly was the heir to his political kingdom, but back when he died, she was too young to accept the throne. If he'd only stayed alive longer. Molly was a lot like him. She quoted him as though he were still her mentor. "Learn all that you can about anything that interests you..." she reminded Gert when Gert went into the seminary, "that's what my dad always said." Molly'd be in politics soon. All the publicity about her cases. It had to help. Too bad the mayor couldn't see her now.

Molly talked about him as though he could. As though he were just across town. As though he'd never died.

Of course, Gert wondered if that was why Molly liked Joe.

Nuns taught Greek. Nuns taught Oedipus. Couldn't fault them. Couldn't say they didn't teach the bright girls about father figures. Molly should have learned. Gert should have been bright enough to remind her. Instead, she'd danced around the issue.

"I don't want him to make you feel old, Molly," Gert had said.

Molly was defensive. "Something wrong with the age difference?"

"Does he make you feel old?"

"On the contrary. It's like I'm eighteen and going to the Prom with the captain of the football team. I've never done that, Gert, and I want to."

Molly had wanted a lot. After she finally divorced her first husband, she wanted a lot. There was this black guy. A guy she worked with in the poverty program. There was a time when Molly said she was in love with him. A time when Gert thought Molly wanted to marry him.

"I did," Molly admitted. "He didn't want to marry me. Didn't want to be a minority in his own household."

"And the transvestite?"

"I didn't date him, Gert, he was just my friend. Anyway, we don't know that he was a transvestite for sure."

"You said he was," Gert answered.

"I said he had a wig and a dress in his closet. That's all. Shouldn't be so judgmental." Now Gert wished she'd been more judgmental. Wished she'd stopped Molly from practicing that brand of liberalism of hers that required her to trust everyone, to

35

accept every behavior, to allow every difference. It reminded Gert of a Proust character, a woman who walked into danger without noticing. On the surface, they were different, that woman and Molly. On the surface they were the opposite. Proust's woman was afraid of everything. Molly was afraid of nothing. But in the end, they came around to the same place. If you're neurotic enough, all situations seem threatening. And you cope by ignoring every threat. No alarms. You pay no attention to any alarms. Signals don't count any more. You stop noticing danger. And it was the not noticing that made Gert think of Molly.

It was the not noticing that was the same. Nothing caused Molly any alarm. Molly had abandoned every intuitive fear. But she couldn't abandon a cause and she wouldn't consider the possibility of a rejecting a human being. For Molly, there was no one undeserving of her love. She did not understand that there were people she did not have to care for. People she did not have to like. People who might be dangerous. Molly opened her arms to everyone, first the outcast, then the oligarch.

Ten years before, Gert had asked Molly, "Is he straight? This judge, is he straight?"

"As an arrow," she answered. "Fifty-five years old. Pillar of the community. An establishment man."

"He's the white male power structure," Gert said.

"Last year I couldn't even say that phrase," Molly laughed.

"And now you're going to marry it."

When Molly married, she kneaded herself into the parched history of her husband's life. She accepted her yoke as a wealthy man's wife as freely as she had taken on the crusade to save Allan-What's-His-Name. And until now, Gert had not remembered her original apprehension about Joe. He had seemed to give Molly what she wanted. And Molly had never said otherwise.

The plane was starting to land. Gert dropped the almonds into her purse. When the wheels touched ground, she pulled her duffel bag out from under the seat. She grabbed her coat and hat from the overhead shelf and began walking toward the exit before the other passengers clogged the aisles. She was the first one off the plane. She wound her way, back and forth, through what seemed an interminable serpentine walkway from the plane to the waiting area. There was no sign of Molly. No Jimmy grinning and waving. Nobody she recognized. It gave her an odd feeling. Made her want to rush. Told her it was time to hurry. No more patience. No more contemplation. No more waiting. Gert was walking back and forth, trapped by an aluminum fence, no choice but to zig-zag slowly through the maze. But halfway through, she couldn't stand it any more. Halfway through, she lifted her boot and hurdled a metal barrier that had been containing her. First she leapt over one. Then another. Then another. And when she had jumped them all and was free of the corral, she bolted and ran.

No one was waiting at baggage claim. No one at the ticket counter. No one answered the page. Gert let the phone ring, twenty times, at Molly's before she hung up and hailed a cab.

And now, as they drove close to Molly's house, it looked empty. It was big and square and brown. From the street, it was dark. Shades were pulled over every window.

Gert told the cab driver to turn into the driveway and keep going, all the way back. Two cars were parked there, a small one and an Olds. The Olds had snow all over it. But the small one's windshields were nearly clear, as though someone had left it only moments before and gone inside.

"When did it stop snowing?" she asked the driver.

"Not sure," he said. "An hour maybe, forty minutes or less..."

Gert paid the driver. She was going to ask him to wait, in case they weren't home. But now, with cars in the driveway, it looked like Joe and Molly were there, behind the silly closed blinds. She gave the driver a tip and headed for the house. Funny they didn't come meet her plane.

She pressed her finger on the doorbell and then she realized the door was open. Wide open, except for the heavy glass storm. And that wasn't hooked. Gert walked into the kitchen. Molly must have gone in right ahead of her.

"Molly?" she called.

Normally, the door would have been bolted. Joe was like that. Joe was a security nut. A watchdog, always pacing from front door to back, pulling shades, bending a sliver to look out. But no more than that. No windows open. No doors.

That's what he was doing the last time she visited. Two years ago. When Gert came for the high school reunion. Joe was pacing. Peeking from behind a locked door. Looking for something or someone. Uneasy.

"Concerned," Joe had said that night. "Worried you two were having car troubles."

"Sure," Molly had said and brushed by him, into the kitchen.

"Lonely?" Gert had asked, meaning to tease him. She thought he liked her teasing. He'd always liked her teasing. He blushed and pouted and pretended to dab a tear from his eye.

"You're a dear to be lonely for your wife," Gert had said in mock admiration. And they laughed.

But Joe locked the door behind them. Double locked it with a dead bolt. Always locked the door. Even the next morning, a warm morning, sun shining. Gert could smell flowers and wet earth, she could smell spring from the open window in her bedroom. But when she went down to the kitchen for coffee, Joe was sitting there in the dark. Shades pulled. Windows locked. Doors bolted. House-bound.

"City," he's said. "Town's a big city now. Can't be too careful."

That's why Gert didn't like the door being unlocked now. Unless Molly were right there, the door wouldn't have been open. Joe would have locked it. He would have insisted. Something felt wrong.

She called again, "Molly!" There was no answer.

Gert went outside to ask the driver to stay. But the cab was gone.

She turned around and went back into the kitchen. It was dark. Gert flicked on the light.

"Molly? Joe? Jimmy?"

There was still no answer. She called louder, "Where are you guys? It's Gert."

The house was damp and cold, as though the heat were off, or the door had been open all afternoon. And there was a strange, familiar smell. Musky. Wild.

"Molly?" she called again.

In the living room, she switched on a lamp next to the couch and looked around. Mail on the coffee table. Books, probably Jimmy's, on the telephone stand. On the floor next to it, a brown grocery sack and a briefcase.

"Jimmy, Joe. Hey... anybody home?" Gert shouted up the stairs. There was light in the upstairs hall, or in one of the bedrooms. From the foot of the stairs, she could see a small strip of light running across the carpet. Gert shivered. Chilly and damp. They ought to leave the thermostat higher in the winter. It was going to take hours to warm the place up again. Not to mention the scent.

38

"Mol?" She walked up the stairs, "Molly, you up here?"

She followed the strip of light to a bedroom door, open just enough to release a splinter of light into the hall.

Gert was uncomfortable, to say the least. To be invited to a friend's home, begged, entreated, really. Then ignored at the airport as though she weren't expected. Having to let herself in. Having to barge into the house, and now into the bedroom. She was very uncomfortable. She rubbed her hands together. They were icy. Like the air.

"Jimmy?" she said quietly, "Jimbo?"

No answer. She reached for the knob. Her fingers were stiff. What was she dreading? Was it the quiet? That was it, wasn't it? The room was too quiet. The house was too quiet. She didn't want to open the door.

"Molly?" she whispered. There was no response. Gert stood outside the room, waiting. Hoping for a sound. A noise that gave her reason to go in. Or reason to stay out. But there was none. Only silence.

Finally, she pushed the door and took one step inside.

And that's when she recognized the damp, musky odor. It was the wild smell of hunting season. The strong, musty scent of ducks draining in the back hall. The cold, wet breath of blood.

There was a man, stretched out across the king-sized bed. His blood was all over the wall. She was sure it was Joe.

Gert raised her hand in blessing, but what power had she against this? She looked at the figure on the bed. Was she trying to communicate between the living and the dead, or between the dying and the eternal? She didn't know. But words came quickly to mind, "... May your rest be this day in peace, and your dwelling place in paradise." She left him then, and walked to the other rooms. Slowly, she opened every door. Every bedroom. Every closet. The attic. Downstairs. She went through the kitchen. Out the back door. Into the driveway.

It had started to snow again.

THE CHORUS

Sandra Gens had never been on television. She was a newspaperwoman. Always had been. Now, as they clipped a small microphone to her blouse, she wondered how good an idea it had been to say "Yes" when they invited her to do guest editorials on public TV.

She crossed her legs at the ankles, smoothed her navy wool skirt so that it blended into to the dark grey couch, and took a deep breath.

"Relax. We're low key here ..." said a fellow wearing ear phones. He was connected to somewhere back in the middle of the studio by a long chord that tethered him like a prized show dog. "Look at the camera with the red light on top."

Sandra looked. Somehow the words she'd typed this afternoon had been blown up to four times their natural size and splayed out across the camera lens.

"Just read, right off the screen, exactly what you wrote," he said. "The words will roll along with you. Nothing to it."

They told her it wouldn't be any different than writing a column for the newspaper. Sandra wasn't sure.

The host of the show was a balding man who had once been an anchor on the ABC affiliate in Fargo. He was sitting at a desk about six feet to Sandra's right. She could hear him talking now about the abuse cases, about Molly Stuart, about Sandra Gens and how she was going to use her newspaper column from now on to put the abuse issue in focus. The host explained that Sandra was doing an extra column this week — a TV column — for his show.

That was it. She heard her name again and the word "Chorus" and saw the red light flash on above the camera. The fellow with the earphones wound up like a baseball pitcher and after one majestic swoop of the arm he aimed his fist directly at her. Without making a sound he mouthed the word "Go!"

"DATELINE," Sandra said, "ST PAUL," and then she began to read her column as it rolled across the front of the lens:

LIVE:

In my column this morning I chastised Molly Stuart for lacking trust, trust in you, in me, in the foster homes of this community — lack of trust in the fabric of American Society.

My theory was that most of us are good, gentle souls who like kids... and who wouldn't stand by and let anything bad happen to them. After all, that's what America is all about, isn't it?

Democracy. Love for the underdog. Protection of the little guy. I know little guy means the small businessman, the fellow next door, but I always thought it was a term that could be extended to people who were small in stature, like children, as well.

But I got some interesting phone calls this morning — calls that make me wonder if I'm wrong about the definition of the American Way. These particular callers believe Molly Stuart ought to drop her investigation. One man said he's heard the allegations, and he doesn't believe there's a single incident of abuse that couldn't be reclassified as either "discipline" or "love."

Well, I hadn't had a chance to read the specific allegations, but I have heard Stuart talk — she's been on radio and TV and she hasn't minced a word. In fact, a few days ago her descriptions were so precise on a TV talk show that they covered her comments with a bleep. Sensational? She'd be the first to admit it. Does she overexplain? She says she has to be graphic or the public will never understand what she's talking about.

"You've got to call it what it is," she said on a talk show after they bleeped her description of a particularly unsavory sexual assault.

And in my opinion, what it is has little to do with either "discipline" or "love."

What is it, then? Why can't we reach into our dictionaries and come up with terms that describe exactly what happened to these kids? I think it's because we don't understand the word "abuse." It's too nebulous a word. What is abuse anyway? And, do we all agree that abuse is bad? My dictionary says the word "abuse" comes from two Latin words: ab and uti. Put them together and you get "all used up." And that's the way many of us think of abuse — like using up a bottle of wine on a Saturday night when we should have saved some of it for Sunday. Sure, you misused the wine a little, but after all, it was your bottle of wine to start with, wasn't it?

Transfer that concept of ownership to your family: if you can't abuse your own kids, whose kids can you abuse?

So that's the problem. We hear about the allegations Stuart's making, then we hear this vague word "abuse," and it just doesn't sink in. To that extent, the man who called me this morning was right. There is something wrong with the words we're using. We do need to do some reclassification. We need to come up with the right names for what's going on. But how?

I've got an idea. Let's forget these people are kids for a while. Let's even forget they're Americans. Don't think of them as children in the house down the street. Instead, consider them citizens of a foreign country.

See what words come to mind when you think of them like that.

What do we know about these citizens? They are afraid. Afraid to talk, afraid to admit what happened to them; some of them are even afraid to remember.

Those who do remember tell stories like these:

One was awakened every hour, and subjected to long and bitter harangues that would end only when he would admit to the charges that were leveled against him.

Another was confined to a small, windowless room — no larger than a closet — for hours at a time, deprived of food and air and freedom.

Yet another was forced to walk barefoot in the snow. She was often stripped of all her clothing, not just her shoes.

All of them were coerced into these acts by rulers of the country where they lived, rulers who were extremely large — almost gigantic — and often armed. The rulers used the citizens in sexual

43

experiments, often raping them, sometimes sodomizing them with crude household tools, sometimes forcing them to have sex with animals.

Why didn't these citizens run? Why didn't they leap over the wall? Why didn't they get away? The rulers threatened them, they say. Threatened to harm not only them, but young family members and beloved pets as well.

And where were the good people in this society? There must have been some, even one, who could have helped. They watched, in silence. They stood, and did nothing. They said they may have suspected, but they never really knew.

What words come to your mind when you hear the stories told this way? Totalitarianism? Do you need to be more specific? Communism? Fascism? Nazism?

And what about locking kids in dark cells (even if we do prefer to call them closets), depriving them of food, depriving them of sleep and forcing them to confess to acts they did not commit? Last time I heard about that kind of psychological coercion it was called "brainwashing."

And what do you call foreign tyrants who perform sexual experiments on small children? I call them "war criminals."

And the so-called innocent bystanders — Mom, Grandma, the folks next door

— the ones who say they couldn't do anything to help? Call them what they are too, call them "collaborators."

Think of these children as citizens of a world where a violent gang of brown-shirted bullies hold sway, where the little guys are punished and raped "for their own good." Where the people who are supposed to protect them are tyrants who trample on human and civil rights. And then realize these kids are not halfway across the world. They are here. In America. Home of the free and the brave.

If the allegations these kids are making are true, they need more than Molly Stuart. They need Amnesty International. And they need all of us to take another look at what we call "discipline" and "love."

The man with the earphones asked Sandra to stay on the set until the host had introduced the next segment. It was going to be a taped piece, he said, and she could stand up and leave as soon as the tape rolled. They always did it that way so the TV audience wouldn't see a guest leave. Then he handed her a folded page from a tan memo pad. It was a message from her newsroom. "Call," it said. "Urgent. Call." It was unusual. They didn't usually try to track her down. Sandra hoped she hadn't done too badly on TV. Had she? Maybe they simply wanted to tell her she did well. Why else would they send her a note? She put it in the pocket of her skirt and waited until it was all right for her to go.

CONFITEOR

Molly was standing outside, across the street from her house, in that little park with the ice rink, because she did not want to go back inside. She had been in there and had seen something she did not want to see again, something that had soiled her long white coat, blotched it with stains, something she could not remember. She had a feeling she had missed something, that there were things she had not recognized, details she had not noticed. Today? Yes, and yesterday, and before. Words she had not heard, or had forgotten, and had no strength to remember. All she wanted to do was to lie down like a child, to fall back into a drift of wind and move her arms and legs until she made the impression of an angel in the air — blowing and drifting air. She looked up at the clouds and floated into the kind of dream that fogs reality and protects its dreamer from the cold horror of truth.

She had watched as Gert went into the house; she'd seen edges of light flicker around window shades; and now, she could see Gert coming down the driveway, walking toward her. And Jimmy — he was running up the Ohio Avenue hill. And there were red lights flashing from the bridge, a squad car, moving slowly toward her, blinking red in a white cloud, darting and rolling, as thought it were in no hurry, as though it had stopped there, by the bridge; but it hadn't. And when she looked at Jimmy again, he was skipping, dancing across the ice, skating up the hill, sliding back, coming quickly, yet not arriving. No one was arriving. Gert took large, giant steps, slicing through the snow in slow motion, yet she did not move. Everyone was hurrying toward Molly and no one was arriving.

Everyone except Joe. Where was Joe? Molly did not know where he was.

All afternoon, she'd been wondering why he'd left her.

Why had be been so angry? Had she said too much? Until now, she hadn't wanted to answer those questions, hadn't wanted to know; not if it was going to be bad; she had wanted time with Gert, no interference, peaceful time, no problem. No reaction to Joe, no more reaction. That's the way it was for her lately anyway;

things took time, she didn't always feel things right away, hours, sometimes days came between his anger and her response. But now, something was happening, something was forcing her to remember why he left.

It was the new little boy, wasn't it? It was his talk of sacrifice. She could not press it back any more, that must have been what happened, why he ran away. My God, were they really killing kids? Sure, she'd been prepared to believe the little boy; she had always been prepared to believe the children, but this time something inside, some kind of hope, had made her hang on to the idea that maybe it hadn't happened yet, maybe the child had only been threatened. It always took time to get children to explain, time and patience while they danced in silence and shame. Maybe there was still time for hope.

Hope, she felt it, even at lunch, even when she told Joe what she dreaded might be true.

"These are the kind of people who end up killing kids," she'd claimed. "Good God, Joe, these people would sacrifice kids!"

She shouldn't have been talking about it, it was too early; there was still a chance the little boy's parents were only trying to frighten him, to control him. Some scare. Some parents. They were animals. And Joe kept claiming they were innocent, all of them, completely innocent.

"Love kids too much," he'd said. "They're good people who love kids too much. That's all they did..."

How could he be so wrong?

"Normal stuff. That's what they did, normal stuff for a parent, like bathing their kids, and you want to put them in jail for it."

She had been silent a moment, then she began to repeat a litany of accusations made by her children, her witnesses.

"Not baths, Joe," she said, "first it was fondling and then it was games — you remember, I told you about the one they called the fire hose game — what a game, let daddy urinate on you."

"Come on," he said, "I know where that came from, some kid just surprised his dad in the bathroom or something and one of your social workers twisted the whole thing around."

"I have a ten year old, Joe, who's mom and grandma make him copulate with them; and I have babies that have to take their fathers in their mouths — I have a two year old with gonorrhea-infected gums."

"Checked that kid's older brother for clap?" he was laughing.

47

"Maybe the brother did it. Why believe the kids and not the parents?"

"I have an infant with anal fissures."

"Diaper rash," he said.

"They say their parents all get together on Sundays and dress up in white robes. And one day they killed a pet dog."

"And you believe that kind of fantasy?" he said. "You don't have any evidence."

"What about an entire family of kids, sodomized with a wooden spoon? We found that fucking spoon in the kitchen drawer!"

"Cool it, will you?" Joe looked around. "You talked that way on TV last week and they blacked you out. You can't talk like that Molly, not in public."

"If I don't talk that way, nobody takes me seriously." Molly thought about the time she tried to be polite, tried not to talk that way to the city council. Explain what you mean by abuse, they insisted. So she told them she was going to skip specific details because the children's stories were disturbing to many people. She didn't want to spell it out, not in public. She told them she'd explain it all when it was time, in court; she would, of course, explain it all, but not there, not that day, not in an open council meeting.

That's when the council turned against her. "Every parent does something that could be called wrong," said the councilman from the East End. "You gonna put every parent in town in jail?"

"Nobody should take this seriously," Joe smiled at her when she talked about it at lunch. "Of course they don't take it seriously. Nobody should."

"You should!" she must have been screaming at him, "Joe, these people are destroying children."

He stood. His face was grey. "You're crazy," he said, and he turned his back on her.

"No. I'm not. I've got evidence," she knew she was exaggerating, but she had to make him understand; she thought he'd believe her if she told him things that were even worse. "I'm going to prove they're killing more than dogs. I'm going to prove they're killing kids!"

Joe spun around and glared at her. "Stupid," he yelled at her, "You are a stupid and dangerous woman."

He left quickly, and when Molly called his chambers they said he was gone for the day.

But not then, not at the courthouse, not all afternoon, not until she reached home had Molly allowed herself to believe that the worst might actually be true. Now she stood in the snow and, more to herself than to anyone else, she murmured, "I am so sorry."

She took her gloves out of her pockets. How had she forgotten to put on gloves? She slipped them over her hands. She was cold.

A few minutes before, the woman next door had pulled Molly into her kitchen and called Jimmy's best friend down on Ohio Avenue and told him to come home, without telling him why. And then the neighbor dialed the police and handed Molly the phone and left the room quickly. The neighbor reminded Molly of women at church when Molly was young. The ones who wore woolen scarves, tied under their chins, and — when they prayed their rosaries — knelt far, far away from the confessionals lest they be guilty of overhearing another's sins. The neighbor kept her distance too, while Molly talked on the phone, as though Molly were speaking to the police of sins the woman did not dare to hear.

As soon as the calls were made, Molly ran out of the neighbor's house. She ran across the street to stand on the frozen rink, to be where she could see, where she had seen Gert's cab arrive and leave, where she could breathe. The air was cold and it was snowing again, wet snow in Molly's hair, but it didn't bother her; she could barely feel it. She glanced from Jimmy to Gert to the police car and she wondered which of them would reach her first.

And where was Joe?

Crisis was spilling all over: sirens were wailing and lights were flashing and neighbors were looking out their windows and privacy was being dumped in the street; and Molly still did not remember where her husband was. Besides that, she had not taken the time to be concerned about how he was going to react. That was another thing that wasn't normal — Molly always worried about how he would react, what he would say, what he would do. He had that kind of power.

Molly cupped her hand just above her eyebrows to keep the snow off her face. She strained to see across the street, to see through the little window in the front door.

There. She thought she saw him, in the window, separating the two lace panels, peaking out. She could feel him looking at her; she knew he could see her. She supposed he'd even seen her turn into the driveway in Wallblom's Datsun, just like the night she brought Gert home from the reunion. Molly imagined Joe pacing back and forth until she finally got there, then she could see him unlock the deadbolt and open the heavy inside door, leaving the storm shut, standing there, waiting for her.

He was there.

Thick glass panels protected him from the blowing snow.

It was Molly who stood outside, letting the cold, wet flakes seep into her coat and soak through her boots, standing there, looking at Joe — Joe who was in the door, Joe who was there, Joe who was ... Watching.

He was taller than usual; it must have been the angle — he was higher. Molly would have to walk up the steps in the front yard and on the porch to get to him, but it was Joe, all right. He was wearing his navy cashmere sweater and a pair of jeans — the faded ones. And there was light shining down from behind him inside the house — light that bounced off the glass in the storm door. It bounced and reflected all the blue in Joe's clothes back up into his hair so that when Molly looked at him from her spot across the street, his face and his eyes and his teeth and his hair were all shining. To Molly, he was all silver and shining.

The house that seemed built around him was big and strong and square, sturdy, brown and brick. It looked to Molly as though it ought to have been safe.

Gert thought it was. She used to call it chocolate, a chocolate cake, she said last time she was there, a wonderful warm chocolate cake. And she pointed at the capitol and the cathedral across the river, all lit up, and she said they were show-offs with their flood lights in the night.

"You ought to put candles on your chocolate house and shine right back at them," Gert had said.

The house was shining now, couldn't Gert see it? Joe was glittering in the doorway. He was as bright as the gold gilt horses on the capitol, as white as the cross at the top of the cathedral's green copper dome. The house didn't need candles.

"Happy house," Gert had called it two years before. She thought it was happy because it had high ceilings. Gert liked high ceilings and Mexican tiles and white walls — every wall inside the house was white, clean and fresh and white.

"Immaculate," Gert had said.

Immaculate except for the swirly spots by the front and back doors, scuff marks in the polyurethane on the hardwood floors.

Gert found them. Joe's, she said, from his loafers, from his pacing, twirling, rushing to the back. Gert joked about it. She teased him. Said it was cute of him to be lonely. Cute and sweet and dear.

But Molly knew he'd actually been angry. Joe didn't like being home with Jimmy, said the boy made fun of him, said the boy didn't respect him, didn't obey. The boy was a sneak, a liar, don't believe him, he said, no matter what the boy says. He's stealing money; he's spoiled; he's a rotten kid. Molly was fooling herself, he said, Jimmy was no good. When Joe was his age, he had a job. Jimmy, he said, didn't even know how to wash his hands.

Power. Joe had power over her, and Molly didn't know why. With other people, she was the strong one, but as long as Molly could remember, Joe had been able to frighten her, to shame her, to make her cower. She couldn't believe she hadn't worried how Joe was going to react: everything was a mess in there, in the house; and he wasn't going to like it, not at all.

"Filth," Molly could hear him screaming at her, "I can't live in this filth."

Sometimes Molly got up in the middle of the night to clean, to make sure nothing was out of place, to make sure Jimmy hadn't left anything out of place, because Joe had power over Jimmy too.

He could scare Jimmy too, like when Jimmy left soap in the bath tub instead of in the dish and Joe took every bar and hid it and said the boy was wasteful and needed to be taught; he said he would teach the boy.

Molly remembered Joe's voice, how it sounded that day when he was teaching Jimmy about soap; it was soothing, almost like a lullaby.

There were upstairs, alone, in Jimmy's room, the boy and his father, when Molly heard the tenderest of tones. It was rare, lately, for him to be kind to the boy, so rare she went upstairs to listen, pleasing sounds, sweet sounds. But as she stood there, the words she heard did not fit together, they did not fit the sound.

He said boys needed to be embarrassed, publicly. He said if he ever found him wasting soap again he would force him to go unwashed. He said there was nothing he would enjoy more than letting the world see what a fool, an ignorant, wasteful, dirty fool the boy really was. He said he loved the boy. And he would love seeing the boy shunned by his friends because his clothes were filthy and his body was fowl.

Rhythmically, the father insulted the son. There would be no more baths, there would be no more showers, there would be no more washing before dinner. And there would be no more dinner at the table for such a filthy boy. Low tones, soft tones, he was nearly singing. The boy was lucky, he was saying, and the father was pleased. It made the father happy to show him the proper way.

Molly opened the door. Jimmy had turned away from his father. Joe was staring out the window, the sun glaring back into his grey eyes. When he saw Molly, his left leg trembled, a single spasm from his waist to his foot, and it went rigid. Then he stood and, as though he didn't notice he was limping, he left the room.

And that evening, when Molly wanted to shower, she had to beg for soap, she ended up begging for soap. Joe said she should have taught her son, said Jimmy's waste was her fault because she should have taught him. Then Joe let her use one bar, and, as soon as she was done, he took it back so the next morning she had to beg all over again.

Of course, she bought more soap — brave and private soap, hidden for herself and her son — and she told Jimmy to keep it secret, to wash his body in secret, because Molly could not convince her husband that the child had not meant to be wasteful of soap.

"Defiant," is what Joe said he was. Same thing he would have called Molly if he'd known about her secret soap. Same thing he called her when she bought food he didn't like. Fast food, tasteless food, wrong food.

Molly looked around her at the snowy ground, at her empty hands, no grocery bag, no wine, no bread. She had left it in the living room. Oh, God, in there, with Joe. She remembered the time he kicked the loaf of bread across the kitchen to show Jimmy his mother had bought the wrong kind. Would he do that again, with Gert there?

Gert wouldn't put up with that. No matter how soft his voice, Gert would confront him. Gert would tease him; Gert wouldn't let him off the hook, or her. She wouldn't let Molly off the hook either.

"Don't you know what's going on here?" Molly was sure Gert would ask.

She would ask because she would know, like Molly knew, deep down. She would know how sad Molly was, how angry

Molly was, how awful it was to beg for a bar of soap.

"How can you do the kind of work you do and ignore what's going on in your own home?" That's the kind of question Gert would ask.

"We're all right," Molly had answered before, she always answered that way when her mother asked how they were. And Molly's mother always accepted the answer. But Gert wouldn't. Gert would make Molly wonder if they really were all right.

"What are you waiting for?" Gert would say. "Do you have to wait until he does something worse to you and Jimmy?"

Wasn't that what she had been afraid of? When she heard his lullaby, his sweet tones of chastisement, his loving teaching about soap, wasn't that the question she had really ignored? Joe, the same as those other people, planning to do something worse to Jimmy. Or was it already done?

Jimmy wouldn't say. Jimmy said nothing. He was silent, as silent as the boy who pointed at the photograph on Molly's desk. Jimmy locked his door now, surrounding himself with solitude, with stillness, with silence.

"I never touched you or your sissy boy," Joe had said to her the night Gert called. "What did you tell that goddamned woman?"

Nothing. She had told Gert nothing.

"So fucking sure of yourself, think you're the only good parent there is. Why don't you quit sticking your nose up other people's business and stay home with your sissy kid yourself? I'll tell you what that would do, make you see how your precious Lord Fauntleroy treats me. Why don't you open your eyes and see how your pretty boy treats me?"

She saw. Jimmy tried to avoid his father. That's all. When he could, Jimmy went upstairs and shut the door. That's all.

"Maybe some smart attorney ought to charge you with neglecting your own kid," Joe said.

But nobody would accuse Molly of neglecting Jimmy, no matter how busy she was. Even when she brought work home, she waited to do it until after Jimmy went to bed. She helped with homework, she drove him to hockey games. She was the most available parent she knew. And lately, since Jimmy seemed to make Joe so angry, Molly had the school bus drop Jimmy downtown. Since Joe had been leaving work early, Molly and Jimmy had taken a cab home together four times. She wasn't neglecting Jimmy. She didn't have time for neglect.

Molly wiped her eyes with her right hand. Tears, blackened by mascara, stained the fingertips of her beige suede glove. She kicked at the snow with her boot, again and again until she could see herself making a little hole. She had been sad for a long time. She had let herself be very sad.

"Why are you always thinking of yourself?" a priest had asked her back in college.

And he'd probably say she was doing it again, thinking only of herself, small, bitter, petty thoughts, angry thoughts. Perhaps the priest was right.

Joe always said it too, said she never thought of him first, never thought of anybody but herself first. Like in the restaurant, maybe that's what she was doing in the restaurant, thinking of herself, trying to prove she was right, to get the best of him, to win the argument, to win the case, or just to win. The scene came back to Molly again; once more she tried to understand.

"Kevin Schmitt is innocent," Joe had leaned across the table and whispered.

"He's guilty as hell," is what she had replied.

But Joe claimed it was all an ego trip for Molly.

"Who do you think you are, parading around the courthouse expounding on the law?"

Molly said she was a prosecutor and child abuse was a crime.

"You think your crazy idea of child abuse is right? None of those defendants had done anything wrong."

She shouldn't have told him about the new little boy, but she had to make him understand.

"Love kids too much. That's all they did..." he said. "...social workers twisted it..."

He didn't understand. Molly had to make him understand. He had to understand.

"Good God, Joe," she had answered. "These people are even sacrificing kids..."

"You are a stupid woman, Molly," he had yelled at her as he left, "a stupid and dangerous woman."

That priest in college would have told Molly to run after Joe, would have told her to follow him. Go. Catch him. He's your husband. But she was ashamed. Too ashamed to go.

Back, across the street, Joe was there again, in the door. She could see him. She wasn't imagining him there, light flashing between him and the door; he must have been real because he wouldn't go away; she couldn't make him go away.

He had something in his hands — soap, all the soap. He threw it in the air and let it fall to the ground and there was a spark when it hit the floor because the soap was all shiny, shiny and silver, like Joe.

"That's enough," Molly cried out. "You can't do this any more," she cried, "Joe, this time I called the police."

But she could see he didn't care. He was still there, in the door, waiting — waiting like she was, for the police, for Jimmy. It made Molly angry and she shouted at him again.

"Why did you have to do this?" she yelled. "Do you think you're God?"

She heard nothing in return but Jimmy's voice in the distance calling, "Mom, are you all right?" and she was ashamed again. This time she was ashamed for not having taken her child away from his father a long time ago.

That thought was formed without sound, that shame was only a feeling, but across the street, the silver ears heard and the silver lips grinned and laughter tumbled out of the silver mouth. Then the shining figure spun around and disappeared from the door.

She supposed he left shiny scuff marks on the floor, glistening, swirling stains like the other time, when he scratched the floor, and she got out of bed in the middle of the night and went down to the kitchen. There was furniture polish and a rag under the sink and she took it to the living room and, on her hands and knees, she wiped away the marks. Then, like she did every other time he had frightened her, she went back to him. Now, as she looked down the street, she saw the squad car drawing closer and closer to the house, and she wondered if the police would let her clean away the stains this time.

Then she clapped her hands together to shake the snow off them, left the ice rink and the little park, and ran toward Jimmy, to reach him before the police did. The squad car stopped in front of the house, its lights illuminating the entire street, bright white, bright red. Molly and her son stood in the beams of light; she hugged him and she cried. She patted him on the back and she kissed his blue ski cap and she kissed the snow that covered it and she kissed the straight blond hair that jutted out at the edges.

"Mom," he said, "everything's okay."

Gently, Molly pushed him an arm's length away and she looked at him. The boy was their miracle, hers and Joe's, together, they had created life. She clutched Jimmy back to her. When he rested his head on her shoulder, she hugged him again.

"I'm sorry," she whispered, meaning to talk only to Jimmy. But she knew after she'd said it that she was talking to Joe as well.

KYRIE

One quick glance told Gert it was suicide, but she didn't know when it happened. Before Molly got home, she supposed. Although nobody was getting straight answers from Molly. How long had she actually been there? And Jimmy, did he know anything?

There were questions, but this wasn't the time to ask them. Morning would be better. Right then, all she wanted was to get Molly and Jimmy out of there. Out of the house, through the crowd of reporters, away from it all. Home — to Molly's mother's. She called Molly's mother and explained what happened. Told her she was putting the two of them in a cab. Sending them home. Right away.

Then she dialed information for Yellow Cab's number and called a taxi. Half hour wait, they said, bad roads, icy. It was right after she hung up the phone that she heard the noises upstairs. Doors slamming. Voices. Molly and Lieutenant Cook.

"My husband's alive!" Molly's voice was airy, almost childish.

Gert took the steps three at a time.

Lieutenant Cook turned to see her bounding up the stairs. As he moved, Molly reached around him. She turned the knob and opened the door and would have gone inside, but he grabbed her by the arm and held her.

"Close the door," he shouted and someone slid it shut from the other side.

The lieutenant was a man in his forties. Gert found him good looking from a distance. But something about his grooming bothered her. Pristine. Over-preserved. Shaved too close, for one thing. And his hair, it was cut extremely short around the ears. His cologne was heavy and sweet. He towered above Molly as the two of them stood outside the bedroom.

Gert put an arm around Molly. Her white wool coat was stained with blood and vomit.

"I'm ashamed I was sick, sick a while ago," Molly said. "I guess I made it worse. I think I saw him. Can I see him? Talk to him again?"

57

"Of course," Gert started to open the door.

"Downstairs!" The detective's order was brusque. He was trying to force them out of there. Old argument from authority. Gert didn't like it. Never liked it. She'd been eye to eye with authority before and she knew it wasn't always possible to win. She also knew she'd have to act as though the opposite were true. As though there were no doubt that she would win.

"I'm a priest," she said and reached for the door again. "I am going to say a prayer for him."

"Nobody's going in there," the lieutenant answered.

"His wife certainly has a right to see him and have a prayer said for him."

"Get her downstairs," he said. "Now."

It was no use. The policeman was blocking the door with his body. No sense wasting rational energy on him. She'd have to find another time to give Joe the last rites. Molly had tears running down her face. Gert took her hand. It was clammy. She tugged gently and led her down the stairs, toward Jimmy. He was there in the front hall. He'd been there a while, watching his mother and the policeman. He was silent. Hadn't spoken a word since they'd come inside. Just stood there, watching. Too much for him, Gert supposed. Too much for any nine year old.

"Hey, let's go, Jimbo," she said, "You must be starving. Let's go find some food."

She led them to the kitchen and sat them down at the table. Jimmy was satisfied with a glass of chocolate milk and a peanut butter sandwich. For Molly, she made thick, black coffee.

Gert opened the curtains on the windows by the driveway and pulled up the shade. There were reporters out there. Must have been a couple TV reporters standing in front of cameras and those glaring, white lights. Jimmy went to the window and looked out. One of the lights flashed past him and spilled onto the kitchen floor.

"They're taking my picture," he said.

"Then maybe we better shut them out," Gert said and she pulled the shade down once more.

It didn't seem like Molly had noticed. She sat with her feet under her, her elbows on the table, her chin in her hands. She was staring at the walls. Talking about her white walls.

"They weren't always white," she said. "They used to be vines and flowers and tweeds..."

Sounded like someone talking in her sleep. Everytime she emptied a cup of coffee, Gert filled it again. Come on, Molly. Wake up.

"Wallpaper leaves stories," Molly said, "you redo a house, you're some kind of archaeologist. Steam off the tweeds, there's the age of stripes, scrape them away, here come the vines... All the families that used to share this piece of earth... Their lives... their histories... Scrape your fingers against the walls, you can find them all, still here."

Jimmy finished his sandwich and began to wander back and forth, from the front door to the kitchen, pausing, pulling up an edge of shade, looking out at the reporters, looking for the cab.

"But I didn't do that here. A man scraped our walls, with a machine; we just hired a man. I didn't do anything," Molly said, "so that's our story, nothing there, just say what color, that's all I did, say white; I should have done more."

Gert still wasn't sure what Molly was talking about. She wanted to get her away from here. Either that, or let her see her husband's body. Molly didn't seem to understand that he was dead. She needed to find out. To say the word. Suicide.

Come to terms with it. Molly was acting like Joe was still alive. Talking about him. Talking to him. It seemed cruel, but upstairs Gert had actually wanted Molly to look at his corpse. Thought maybe that's why Molly went up there in the first place. Why she was dodging around Lieutenant Cook. Intuitive drive to discover reality. Probably would have snapped out of it by now if the cop had let her see the body. Stupid man. Had no reason to keep them out. Gert wanted to shake him. Shake Molly. Make Molly understand. Gert went to the refrigerator, poured orange juice into a glass, and set it in front of Molly.

"Drink," she said.

"I can peel paper, Gert. I could have coated my fingers in paste," she put her hands together and looked at them, then she rubbed them — one against the other — almost as though she were cleaning glue from them, "mingle myself with people who used to be; mix my work, my sweat, it would be better; he would be happy, we would be..." she smiled. "In Peru I built a mud brick house and worked until my hands bled into the earth..."

Molly's talk was disjointed, vaporous, but it was beginning to have a haunted logic to it. She was describing something she still longed to share with a lover she would not admit was dead.

59

"Better to suffer over this house, to let him see me do that, work and sweat and feel and enjoy..."

It was not property. Not simple physical property she was talking about. No. Molly was talking about walls and paint and paper and paste, but she was talking about more than that.

About mystical equity in more than a house. An equity of sacrifice. Wishing she'd mingled her own blood with the plaster and paint. One with the house. One with Joe. Sharing his story.

"It's here... " Jimmy ran in from the living room. "Let's go, Mom, Let's go."

Gert planned to stay there at the house, after Jimmy and Molly were gone. To hear what the police would say. What they would say to her and what they would tell the reporters. Gert had to find out. She also had to pray.

She hadn't intended to let the lieutenant know Molly was going to leave. Get her out of there. Keep her away from his red tape. But the policeman must have heard Jimmy or seen the cab roll up the driveway. Now he was calling from upstairs.

Gert looked out the window. How could he help but see it? It was all lit up, yellow cab, brilliant under TV lights. The driver beeped. How could the lieutenant help but notice? He called to Gert again from the head of the stairs.

"Ms. Peterson," he was gruff. "Who's the cab for?"

Gert walked into the living room. "Molly and the boy."

"Where're they going?"

"To her folks' house," she said. "Mayor Stuart's old house, you know. You've heard of him, right?"

Lieutenant Cook came down the stairs. "I think she should stay."

He couldn't hold her there. Gert knew that. Wife of a suicide victim. Why would he want to keep her there? This time Gert was not going to let him win. She was going to get Molly out. It was bad for her. Keeping her in limbo.

Gert stood at the foot of the stairs and looked up at the Lieutenant. "She and the boy need rest," she said. "You know where they'll be. I'll give you the address if you want."

Gert turned away from him and walked back toward the kitchen.

"I need her coat," the lieutenant said and followed behind Gert.

"I don't know why you should," Gert spun around. "I don't know if she has another. It's cold outside. She needs to stay

60

warm."

Gert didn't like this man. Something was seething inside of him. Festering. Yet on the outside he was so neat. His wool slacks — just between brown and grey — perfect with his tweed jacket. She had been right when they were upstairs. It wasn't going to be easy to break through his veneer. She'd be lucky if he let her anywhere near Joe. Might not let her in the room. Not even to pray. They walked silently to the kitchen.

Molly was still there, standing by the door. She had taken off the coat and was holding it over her arm, holding it out for the lieutenant. That's the way it always was. Gert questioned; Molly obeyed. When the policeman took the coat, Molly handed Gert a key.

"It's for Wallblom's car," she said, "the Datsun. Would you bring it later?"

Gert nodded. "Of course," she said. She didn't know who Wallblom was. But she wasn't about to engage Molly in a conversation about that right now. That was another thing that could come tomorrow.

Molly went to the closet near the back door and pulled out a ski jacket. It was snug, short at the wrists, probably Jimmy's, but Molly didn't seem to mind.

Gert stood by the door, not wanting to open it until she was sure Molly was going to go directly to the cab. "Don't talk to them, the reporters. Okay? Don't stop at all. Molly, Jimmy, just head straight for the cab. Just walk, as though they weren't even there. Just go."

Light spilled onto them as soon as Gert opened the kitchen door. And it stuck to them as they walked toward the cab. Reporters with their notebooks and cameras and spotlights were right behind.

"Ms. Stuart," a reporter said. "Ms. Stuart, can you tell us what happened here?"

"Ms. Stuart, are you all right?"

"Where is the judge, Ms. Stuart? Is the judge all right?"

Molly turned and looked at the reporters, "He was there, in the doorway. All shiny and bright. I think he's all right," she said. "He's upstairs. They'll let me see him tomorrow. Won't they?" She was looking at Gert now, who had come outside to take her hand and lead her to the taxi.

"Molly, come," Gert said. She fought back the wave of

annoyance she felt rising in her body. Come on, Molly. When's this going to stop? When are you going to understand? "Jimmy's already in the cab, " she said.

Molly slid into the back seat. Gert leaned over and gave Stuart's address to the driver. She knew it like she knew her own. Grew up right next door. Practically the same house. And Irene Stuart was still there. In the old neighborhood. Right now, she'd be there, waiting for them. Probably standing on the screened porch, like she used to. That's how Gert remembered Irene Stuart. On the porch. In the winter. Watching for Molly and Gert to come home when they were kids. Thumping a screen with the side of her fist to clear off the dense snow that had collected on it. Waiting. Patient. Always there. The Stuart house was a good place. They'd be safe.

Gert touched the boy on the knee. "Jimmy," she said, "go straight there, huh?"

"Sure," he answered.

Gert gave Molly a short brush of a hug and shut the cab door. She didn't want to say more than a few words at a time. Reporters everywhere. And what were they going to think of Molly in that trance? They followed Gert with the lights, all the way back to the kitchen door.

"Excuse me, ma'am, can you tell us anything? Has something happened to the judge?"

"The medical examiner is here, can you tell us why?"

"Who are you? Are you a minister or something?"

Gert turned around and faced the reporters. "I'm sorry," she said, and went inside. Good thing she got Molly out of there. Molly couldn't talk to a bunch of reporters. Or a bunch of policemen. Not tonight, anyway. Gert was cold. She went over to the counter and poured herself a cup of the strong coffee she had forced Molly to drink. Then she sat down at the table. Warming herself on the coffee. Sipping. Listening.

Upstairs, they all seemed to be talking at the same time. Buzzing. That detective. And a photographer. And those men with the stretcher. And at least two policemen in uniforms — or four. And a couple in regular suits besides. One must have been the medical examiner. A lot of people. And all of them, talking. Down there, in the kitchen, it all became a hum. She could hear them moving from place to place. Heavy footsteps above her. They must have been moving in a group. First one side of the room, then the other side. Strange. It reminded Gert of the priest and the altar boys and the stations of the cross. Moving together around the church. One with a crucifix, one with a book, one with incense. Talking. Responding. All a hum.

All a buzz. Not disharmonious. High sounds, low sounds. From policemen and men with a stretcher and detectives and a photographer. Talking together. Talking separately. All at the same time. Moving.

There was one loud knock and a man pushed the kitchen door open. He had a black leather bag. It looked like the kind of satchel doctors used to carry back in the fifties.

"Howard Martin, firearms," he said and jerked the satchel as though it were an I.D. "You got a lot of people out there," he said and shut the door behind him. "Where's Cook?"

Gert was on her feet immediately. Out of the kitchen. Up the stairs. Opening the door. Behind Martin. Into the room. Quiet. She was in. Either Cook didn't notice, or he didn't care anymore. She stayed out of the way, by the door.

"Suicide?" Martin asked as he set his bag down on the floor at the foot of the bed.

"I'd say so," said one of the men who'd carried in the stretcher.

"How can you call it suicide when there's no fucking weapon?" Cook asked.

Gert was shocked. She had no idea there was any question how Joe had died. No weapon? Impossible. He had to have killed himself. She was too surprised by the possibility of murder to have noticed the lieutenant's language. Never seemed to notice that sort of thing anyway. Unless someone else called attention to it. Like Martin, the firearms man did. Apparently Cook's choice of words reminded him that he'd come into the room with a woman wearing a roman collar.

"Who's the lady in the preacher's outfit?" he puckered his lips and used his mouth to point toward Gert.

Cook took a deep breath and looked at her, "I gotta ask you to get out of here."

And Gert had to stay. More now than ever. "I'm going to do my job, Lieutenant, you know that," she said. "I need to do the blessing."

It was Martin, not Cook, who answered. "When we're done. I need some time here."

Then he walked close to the body. He knelt down beside it.

63

No one seemed to remember, when he talked, that Gert was still there.

"First impression does look like suicide," he said.

"How in hell can you say that?"

"Experience."

"Bullshit. Your experience is supposed to keep us from accepting a superficial conclusion like that. You're wrong as hell."

"Angle. Look. You got a very close head wound here. Black smudge tattooed on the temple ... Close shot. This wasn't a surprise. Too close. Close enough to be suicide."

"People don't kill themselves and then get rid of the gun."

"You look under the bed?"

"Of course."

"Who's been in here?"

"God knows. The wife. The minister over there, maybe the kid..."

Martin stood and looked at Gert. "You didn't see the gun?"

"I didn't go over there. Just here," she said. "I opened the door, saw the body, that's all. From here."

"Wife was close. That's her coat, covered with blood," Cook said.

"A wife could get close, especially if the guy was sleeping," Martin walked to the little bathroom in the far corner of the room. "Sink looks clean. Anybody use it? Check it for blood or powder. Whoever shot him may have gotten back splash on their hands. Check all the sinks. In case somebody washed."

"Suicides hold the gun right to the temple," Cook said, "and they don't get this powder tattoo. That's another sign he didn't kill himself."

"Not necessarily," Martin said. "They move the weapon sometimes. That's what I'd worry about. The weapon. It means a lot more not being here. Until you know where it went, I'll go along with you. You better call this homicide."

"Fucking murder," Cook said. "You want anything else?"

"Yeah. You guys find a cartridge?"

"Not yet."

Martin told the photographer to get close shots of the powder burns on Joe's temple. And a few more to show there was no weapon near his hand. "It still might be here," he said and gestured toward the body. "Is this who I think it is?"

Cook said yes.

"Wife's the prosecutor, huh? Well, then maybe it is on the up and up. Guy kills himself. The wife goes into shock. Comes over here. Sits on the bed, tries to bring the guy back to life, gun slips under the bed. She gets all covered with blood. Got all the pictures?" he asked the photographer. "Maybe a couple more. Then they can take the body and we can see what's underneath all this..."

Cook was standing next to Gert. "As far as I'm concerned, this is homicide," he said to her, "and you're an important witness, Ms. Peterson."

The men with the stretcher were walking toward the bed. When they got there, they unfolded a large canvas bag. Martin and the photographer stepped out of the way.

"Stop," Gert said. "Wait, I mean. I would like to do what I can."

"You were in here before," Cook said. "Why didn't you do your stuff right away?"

He was right. She hadn't done enough right away. She'd given Joe a cursory blessing and rushed to look for Molly and Jimmy. She realized now it was Molly and Jimmy she was worried about. She thought they were dead. When she saw this, she expected to find their bodies in the other rooms. That's why she went through the whole house. Through every room. Every closet. Perhaps she had thought of murder, but it was murder-suicide she was worried about. And she was convinced Joe was the suicide. Finding Molly and Jimmy alive — it was a surprise.

But Gert didn't answer the lieutenant. She started toward Joe's body until she was stopped. Cook took her by the arm, like he had Molly, and held her back. She was angry.

"You have no reason," she said.

"Homicide's the reason," Cook said. "And your friend the prosecutor is my prime suspect."

Gert could imagine almost anything, but not that. Not Molly. She knew Molly could have been the victim, but not a killer. No way.

"How can you even raise that question?" Gert's voice was loud.

"Prime suspect. And you send 'em off in a cab," Cook said.

Gert looked around at all the men in the room, "You all know her," she said.

Silence.

"She should be beyond suspicion."

Silence again, until Gert realized none of them was looking her way. She meant to clear her throat. Instead, she groaned. The sound, uttered deep inside of her, echoed and reverberated like the speaker on an old stereo. When her voice finally came, it cracked under the strain, "Why don't you understand? She's on your side. Molly Stuart's one of the good guys."

The odd tone made Martin look at Gert. "I don't know where you're from Reverend, but you obviously never heard your friend the prosecutor kind of broke up that fraternity. She put a cop in jail. Just because he didn't follow her orders the way she wanted."

No. Gert didn't know, and Martin could see that. He went on. "She wanted a woman arrested in this child abuse case of hers. This particular officer went out and checked and came back and said there wasn't any grounds for an arrest... Next thing he knew, he was in jail himself."

It made sense. Helped Gert understand the lieutenant's attitude.

"That doesn't apply here," the lieutenant shook his head. "I got a prominent judge who's very dead, and I got a ballistics expert arguing with a preacher about why every cop and lawyer in town should be above the law. Well, you're both wrong. Nobody's getting special treatment here."

He unfolded a piece of stationery. Familiar. Pale blue.

Molly's. Like the paper she'd written Gert's letter on. "And after you send the wife away, Reverend, I find a note that your trustworthy attorney tried to carry out of the house in her coat pocket... that coat, which, we all know, is covered with her husband's blood..."

Gert reached for the piece of blue paper, but he held it back.

"If it's a suicide note, it clears everything up anyway," Gert said.

"This sound like suicide?" he asked. "Listen to what it says here, 'I am afraid for my life. To think the person I love would want to destroy me...' This a suicide note? You think so?"

Gert said quietly, "Who wrote the note?"

Cook ignored her question. "Now," he ordered the men with the stretcher, "Let's get to work. Now."

The men carrying the stretcher moved in front of Gert. There was no more time to argue. She pulled her hand away from the lieutenant and touched the canvas covering that was wrapped around Joe's body. Plain white canvas over a formless corpse. Out of the door. Down the stairs. Gert went with them. She didn't move her hand as she might have from head to foot to lips. She mentioned each sense instead. The eyes. "May the Lord pardon you whatsoever sins you have committed by sight." The ears. "May the Lord pardon you whatsoever sins you have committed by hearing." The nostrils. "May the Lord pardon you whatsoever sins you have committed by smell." The mouth, the lips. The hands, the feet. Some people thought priests were magicians. Supposed to exercise alchemy. Distill all the heavy discord out of human prayer. All the doubt. About Joe. And his death. Produce a sweet melody light enough for God to hear. She had no holy oils to anoint Joe, but she prayed as though she did. "Through this holy unction and the most tender mercy of the creator, may the Lord pardon you whatsoever sins you have committed." God would have to overlook that. Overlook the lack of holy oils. Overlook the heavy flaws Gert always found in her prayers. Weighty prayers. Deep songs. Earthy, like the tone of her own contralto voice. She walked alongside the stretcher. "Lord have mercy." Over and over. "Christ, have mercy." Outside. Gert went with them. Until they reached the van. "Lord, have mercy."

The TV lights followed them, but the reporters stayed back; none of them spoke.

As the men closed the heavy sliding door, Gert repeated the words of the final sacrament. "...may the Lord pardon you whatsoever sins you have committed..."

When she turned around to back inside, Lieutenant Cook was standing behind her.

"You're wasting the Almighty's time," he said.

Gert stared at him.

"You know as well as I do," he said quietly. "You know it, Ms. Peterson. The judge is not the one who needs to be forgiven."

The reporters crowded around the two of them then, circling them there on the snow-covered driveway.

"Will you confirm it was the judge?"

"What happened here Lieutenant?"

"We know it was the judge. Neighbor told us it was the judge. Can't you confirm it for us, Lieutenant?"

"Lieutenant, are you labeling this a suicide?"

"Any chance it was anything else?"

"Any connection to the child abuse ring?"

"Reverend. Excuse me, Reverend, are you part of the family?"

For once Gert was relieved to feel Cook's strong grip on her arm, pulling her away. Cook rushed her past one reporter so fast the woman's notebook was knocked to the ground. He guided Gert to the door and pushed her inside. For a moment, he stood just outside the door.

"Yes, " Gert heard him say. "Yes. The judge. Dead. From a gunshot wound. No. We won't have any additional statement to make this evening. Nothing more tonight. No. Thank you. That's all."

CHORUS

ST. PAUL, Minn. I would like nothing better this morning than to be allowed the gift of silence.

Stillness. Quiet. Peace.

But that is not one of the benefits that go along with my job. Newspaper columnists cannot drape the page with emptiness, even when white space would be a most fitting commentary on the day. I have inches to fill, and I am bound to fill them with words.

I presume that you have read the words on the front page.

A prominent man, from a prominent family, is dead. The man was a pillar of the legal community. A judge. Arbiter of right and wrong. Dispenser of justice.

Husband of Prosecutor Molly Stuart.

Dead. From a gunshot wound to the head.

At this time, no further details are available. But that has not stopped those of us whose business it is to write about such things from filling blank pages in newspapers and empty moments on radio and TV.

Last night I was with a cadre of reporters, all struggling to get the facts — few though there were — in time for both television and newspaper deadlines. In the rush, the following stories were published or aired, some in this newspaper, others on radio and TV:

• An unnamed source from the coroner's office suggested the judge died from a self-inflicted wound.

• Yet another unnamed source, this one from homicide, commented that there may have been foul play.

• A neighbor — there is always one willing to invite reporters in, give them coffee, let them use the phones, and share with them the intimacy that comes from living so close to someone else's grief — a neighbor speculated that the judge's death has sent his wife into a shock so deep that at this writing Prosecutor Molly Stuart still does not believe that her husband, the judge, is dead.

That neighbor helped Molly Stuart call the police last night. She is quoted this morning as saying "Stuart told me she was frightened of her husband. When I reminded her she had just called the police, that he was dead, she said 'No. He doesn't die.' She said he was too powerful to be dead."

• A TV report, making use of a long lens and a strong microphone, aired a scene of Stuart standing outside, pale and shivering in the night. The sound we were treated to was

69

Stuart yelling at the dark windows of her home. "Why did you have to do this?" says her voice. "Do you think you're God?"

* A member of the Lawyers' Professional Committee commented on the TV footage and the neighbor's revelations. He said that Stuart is so deeply enmeshed in a "clinical fantasy" (that is the expression that was used) that she should be relieved of her role in the child abuse cases until she can recover from her own personal tragedy.

Now if I'd rather be silent this morning, why am I repeating all this stuff? And shouldn't I qualify even the word "stuff?"

Okay. "Questionable stuff."

Why? Because I see us all doing exactly the same thing. The writers. The readers. And the wife.

In her horrible pain, Molly Stuart wails in the street. She wails like a woman ought to wail. Unlike Jackie Kennedy — whom we've made the modern archetypal wife — this wife does not stifle her grief. She rants and cries like a mourner in ancient times. She goes so far as to accuse her dead husband of still living... of being an all-powerful God.

Why do I claim we're all doing the same thing? Us, the writers and readers? Well, first of all, I've seen a lot of wailing on TV, and in columns that were supposed to have been reserved for news.

And here's what I think the wailing is all about. We've got a prominent couple here, a judge and a prosecutor, public figures to say the least. We have expectations, and we want our expectations fulfilled. In this society, public figures are supposed to follow certain rules:

* They should be attractive.
* They should be interesting enough for Prime Time TV.
* They should not mind when we, the voyeurs, stand at their windows and peep into their private lives.

Depending on their position in our "Pantheon of Public Figures," we may insist that they:

* provide us with clean air, clean water, and earth pure enough to grow good corn.
* prevent crime, in other words, they should find evil and rout it out.
* teach us the difference between beauty and ugliness, joy and despair.

Most of all, none of these "public figures" is to do anything so ungracious as to exhibit human characteristics like despair, illness or, especially, the ability to die.

We want our heroes immortal, please.

We want our heroes to be gods.

Why are we all alike, all of us, the writers, the readers and Molly Stuart? We all expect our heroes to be divine. We all expect our heroes to live forever. She doesn't want her husband to be dead. We don't want her running through the

70

streets exhibiting grief. We don't want her crying. We don't want her ill. We don't want her weak. We don't want her flawed.

And perhaps that is our great flaw.

Is it asking too much to let Molly Stuart be unheroic for a while? Can we allow her to be weak? Can she be left to her "madness" for a few hours? Can we permit this hero to wail?

It is because I am afraid the answer is "No. We won't allow it," that I wish I had the gift of silence this morning.

I would like to drape this column in emptiness.

Stillness. Quiet. Peace.

Sandra Gens

GLORIA

When Molly woke up that morning, sun was pouring in on her — sun from every window. It was intense white light, heightened as it splashed between the snow below and the clear blue sky above. It came through the windows in giant waves and crashed onto the stark tile floor of the sleeping porch.

The porch was all windows. Three on the north, three on the south, eight stretching across the back on the east. Of all the rooms in Molly's parents' house, that was her favorite — the brightest and airiest. Even the ceramic floor was glazed white. It was one of Molly's father's experiments, an attempt at using solar power, long before it was popular.

Until Molly was fifteen, the room had been her father's den. But after his death, it became an empty space, an extra in a house that already had too many extras for Molly's mother and it stayed that way for years. Books, boxes, storage bags, Molly's corsages from high school dances, the dress she wore in her cousin's wedding, all there, her mother saved everything, a museum or a shrine, everything there, in the empty room. It wasn't until last summer that Molly's mother decided to remodel and rename it. She called it a sleeping porch and set it up as though she ran a Victorian rooming house — a sleeping porch with hanging ferns in the windows and fig trees and rubber plants standing in the corners and a white wicker fainting couch and a matching wicker bed.

"Who's going to sleep on your sleeping porch?" Molly had asked when her mother pushed her father's old desk into a corner and covered it with a lace table cloth.

"Guests," her mother replied.

The night before, Molly had become the porch's first guest. She loved that room, even with the changes; she'd always loved that room.

Gert was curled up across the hall in the bed that had once been Molly's. Jimmy slept in his own room, one his grandmother set up for him when he was just a baby, so he could nap; it always remained his.

Before he went to bed, he had walked out onto the sleeping porch to kiss his mother good night. He said nothing about the tragedy. There had been a tragedy, Molly knew that; that's why they were there at her Mother's, but she hadn't talked to Jimmy about it. She hadn't talked to anyone, except maybe the lady next door. She remembered talking ever so briefly to the lady next door. But not to Jimmy.

"Jimbo," is all she had said to him, "roll up the shades for me, will you?"

"All of them?" he asked.

"All of them," Molly said.

After Jimmy left the room and went to his own bed, Molly had watched the snowflakes grow bigger and softer. Swirling around her until she felt like she was inside a small glass ball, one she'd gotten for Christmas years before, one of those you shake until snow tumbles around and falls at your feet if you're the figure inside. The thought was peaceful and Molly had used it to drift into sleep.

Now it was morning and Molly pulled her comforter around her and propped a pillow behind her and sat up in bed. She breathed deeply, as though she could inhale the light, as though she could suck it in like the aroma of coffee when a new can hisses open. Molly wanted to sniff it and feel her head snap back. She wanted it to taste strong, strong enough to make her shudder — rich enough to force a gasp out of her. She wanted morning light to flash all around her, to force her into the day, to shake her into accepting that she was awake and alert and alive.

Molly had been dazed, she had been dreaming, and now she was worried she wasn't going to wake up. There were people like that, people who did so well at dreaming they lulled themselves into a trance and never came out of it. Shell-shocked. Like Wally in the courthouse coffee shop, still thinking he was in Viet Nam, still talking about hooches. It was madness to get stuck in that kind of bad dream; but it was an alluring madness, so familiar, so comfortable once you got used to it. That's what made her dreaming good, no matter how bad her dreams were. It was normal; it was routine.

That's what Joe said, she was stuck in dreams: bad dreams, good dreams, childhood dreams.

"Always the famous kid," Joe had said. "Play-acting the famous kid. Famous mayor's famous kid..."

"I knew a Stuart once, here in the city ... the mayor,"

It was Joe's dad who said that, right away, when he met Molly,

Joe's dad said it. And it seemed everyone said something like that.

"The mayor's daughter? Is that you? I remember when you were this high," they'd gesture with the flat of a hand three feet off the floor.

"I remember when he was elected. Wasn't that a long time ago?"

Next to Molly's bed on a small table was a photograph of the family, taken that first year he was elected. She was seven, and she was holding the blueprint for her father's famous indoor park for children. That's what people said got him elected the first time, coming up with an idea like that, a park where children could play all winter long in Minnesota.

"A child cannot spend all this life in snow," he had said in one of his speeches, stealing a line from Johnson. It was shortened and adjusted by committee members until it fit on buttons and bumper stickers and "Children Live/ Love Summer" became the slogan of his campaign and "Summer Life" became a synonym for his park — the park with swings and a sandbox and even a kickball field. When they finished building it, Molly was photographed again, this time swinging and playing in the sand and kicking one of the heavy red rubber balls the park supplied for the children of St. Paul.

Molly loved it, being the mayor's kid, the city's first child. That's what her dad used to call her, "Your mother's the first lady," he had said, "and you're the first child." The first lady often tired of all the political jousting. She cared; she wanted her husband to do well in battle with his political foes; but she didn't see the need to be out fighting for votes at her husband's side. Instead, she suited up Molly and sent the child off with her father. Together they went, to picnics and parties and Sunday dinners at churches; and he had called her his campaign manager and his buddy and she loved it.

He liked it too, being in the limelight, being the mayor. Probably would have been governor, a good one, a strangely inventive one, coming up with projects to keep everybody in Minnesota happy, winter and summer. He might be U.S. Senator. Still be in office, maybe, if he hadn't died.

Molly picked up the photograph and looked at it, held it a minute before she set it back on the table. They were happy, all of them smiling — her dad seated at his desk; her mom standing just behind him; Molly, perched on her father's knee, holding the blueprint, grinning like a fool. Joe'd have said that, grinning like a bunch of simpletons. But she liked the picture; she liked being Mayor Stuart's daughter.

"Mayor Stuart's daughter?"

Yes. No matter what Joe thought. It was better than what the nuns used to say in grade school when they insisted on calling her by her formal, baptismal name.

"Mary Stuart?" they'd say, "the Queen of Scots, are you?"

No. She didn't like that one at all. Better to be the daughter of a politician who died of a heart attack than the reincarnation of a beheaded queen.

"Trouble with you is you think you're the heir, the new king, think you're his prince," Joe would say. "Big politician father raised you to be a boy. You don't even know the meaning of the word 'female.'"

Molly pulled her quilt up to her face and rubbed it against her cheek; it was soft and it smelled clean and she was there on the porch, her very favorite place, yet all she could think about were petty fights with Joe. It was a dream, and she wasn't coming out of it; when she tried not to think of Joe, he became all she could remember. His stinging remarks became a chant; intoning, repeating, drawing her into a spell, hypnotizing her. She told herself to forget hard, sad memories, forget madness; she looked out the window at the branches of the old cottonwood tree, wet and black and heavy with crystals of fresh snow. The sky behind was vibrant blue. But everywhere she looked, she saw the outline of Joe's face, as though he were doodled in among the branches, pencil drawings, sketched over and over in all his poses. And he was chanting: telling Molly she was sick, saying she was breaking up families, insisting she was ruining lives; people she accused were innocent, he was saying; children she was trying to protect were lying, like their own child, a liar — don't believe him.

But Jimmy had never said anything.

Never mind, he was humming, don't believe him anyway, his voice was lilting, the boy is stupid, like his mother, he was droning, stupid and dangerous.

Why were such terrible memories a comfort to Molly? They were obsessing her. On the snowy branches she could see Joe's frosty silver breath as his cold words kept her from awakening; in the wind she could hear his heavy gasps. Was he hiding something from her or was he looking for her, circling, pacing, demanding she explain? Explain what? What was the tragedy? She had to wake up and remember.

The door bell rang downstairs and Molly heard it as though it rang right there on the porch. Another of her father's inventions, a sort of crude intercom patterned after one in a congressman's house down in Iowa. Charles Stuart had taken vacuum cleaner hose, yard and yards of it, and run it through the walls from the front of the house all the way up to his den on the second floor. He built in an amplifier, then he covered each end of the system with screen and put it to the test. It worked, and it was still working almost three decades later. No one ever saw any reason to put in buzzers or wires or modernize it; it did the job, let you hear exactly what was going on at the front door. The mayor patented it, even thought about selling it to public servants all over the country, but he was so busy as a politician he never had time to make another one.

"She's the only one," a man's voice came out of the screened hole in the wall of the sleeping porch.

"Only what?" Gert's voice was challenging as it echoed through the tube.

"The first one," said another man.

"Or the last," the original voice said.

"She and the boy," said the other.

"I'll wake her," said her mother. Her voice was exceptionally loud, as though she were trying to remind Molly to listen to the hose in the wall. It sounded the way it used to when irate voters stopped by and her mother tired to speak in a tone so loud her father would know enough to stay upstairs, safe, in his den. Her mother was so good at that. Not just guarding and protecting, but managing, directing; never obvious, but always there, in the wings, making sure things went along as they should.

Molly looked around. Could she stay there? She wanted to hide. Her mother's voice was telling her to hide. Was there a place? She could roll back under the quilt like an invalid, close her eyes and pretend to sleep. Or she could open her eyes and stare wildly, hysterically, at everything and at nothing and they'd leave her alone like they used to leave women after they had suffered a shock. Either way, she wouldn't have to wake up and she wouldn't have to remember. Either way, she would be safe.

Which should she do?

But Molly knew she couldn't do either, couldn't fade back into dreams, couldn't wrap herself in madness.

She slid her legs over to the side of the bed and touched her bare feet on the warm white tile. Then she stood and stretched toward the sun and shivered in its brilliance.

READINGS

Gert walked across the carpeted floor. It felt good, bare toes on the woolen nap. Scratchy but good. She put one foot ahead of the other, bent her knee, stretched. The same with the other foot, the other knee, stretch. Then she reached her hands toward the ceiling, breathed deeply, exhaled, and dropped her hands to her toes, one, two, three. She needed more than that. With all the snow outside she ought to be skiing. Back in Sweetgrass she'd be on her cross countries, halfway into town. Once again she stretched toward the ceiling, breathing deeply. She could see her arms in the mirror, above the dresser. They looked muscled, even a bit tanned. Not bulky or large — not small, not thin. Just comfortable. Comfortable in her own body. Gert felt comfortable lately — as though she were appropriately clothed — in nothing but her own skin. She didn't like getting dressed without working up a sweat and showering it away, but she yanked on her jeans instead. She felt the sticky film of yesterday clinging to her. It dulled her hair and clouded her eyes and coated the taste of the new day. She wanted a bath, soap and shampoo and talcum powder. Not possible, she settled for spraying cologne on her neck and shoulders, a little on her arms. It stayed cool only a second. She tugged on a yellow sweater and then she shook her head, trying to toss the tangles out of her curls before she pulled a large, wide-toothed comb through her hair.

A dab of makeup under the eyes would have to do. The police were on the way, Lieutenant Cook, continuing his surveillance of Molly. How absurd could he be? He must think Joe wrote that note. If that's why he suspected Molly, it was a clumsy supposition. The note was obviously Molly's, not Joe's at all. Anybody could see Molly was the one who was afraid. It was apparent in the letter she sent to Sweetgrass and the way she talked on the phone. Molly was scared. Like a kitten. Backed into a corner. They'd see. Everything would clear up when Molly identified the note.

Shoes. Where were her shoes? Wallblom's keys on the bed, whoever Wallblom was. Duffel bag open with all the cosmetics

78

she didn't have time to enjoy. No tennis shoes? No flats? She'd packed badly. Brought the three-inch heels she loved to wear with skirts, but nothing for jeans, except her boots. And they were downstairs. She picked up the cup and saucer Molly's mother had brought a few minutes before. Just like the old days, with Mrs. Stuart knocking at the bedroom door. When Gert stayed overnight, Molly's mother would wake them. Hot chocolate, it used to be, when they were young. Hot chocolate with a single marshmallow bulging on top. Then, in college, chocolate changed to deep brown coffee and a pitcher of whipping cream. Irene Stuart used to do that for the mayor. Bring him coffee. Nudge him. Get him going. But it was after the mayor died she brought wakeup trays to Gert and Molly. Years after. She must have refilled the trays out of habit. No mayor to get going? No city to groom? No matter. Morning was carried to the girls instead. Like today. Tapping lightly at her door. "Gert?" came the whisper ten minutes before. "Coffee?" Once in the bedroom, Molly's mother said police had been on the phone. Now they were on their way to the house.

"Will you come down?"

Gert rattled the blue china cup, empty, against its saucer. She flicked off the light and walked barefoot to the stairs.

Halfway down, she took the turn in the stairs that led to the kitchen. Jimmy was there, eating toast and jelly, reading the comics. He looked older than nine — crouched over the paper, head hanging, shoulders rounded. Little man, little old man.

"Hi Jim," Gert poured herself another cup of coffee.

Without looking up, he mumbled something into his newspaper.

"Everything ok?" she asked.

"Sure," he answered again without looking up from his page. "Cops are coming. You know that?"

"Yeah, Reenie told me." Reenie was the name everybody called Molly's mother, a name she invented when Jimmy was born so she could dodge the label "Grandma." At first it was meant to be something Jimmy would call her, a word to identify her relationship to him and him alone. But over the years it had become a title for Irene Stuart, one that carried more authority than Christian and family names combined.

"They might want to talk to me again," he said, and for the first time he stared directly at Gert.

"Again?"

Reenie came into the room and it was she who answered, "I'm afraid he answered the telephone this morning when the police called," she said. "They asked him some things, before I got on the line..."

"It's okay," Jimmy said. He went back to his paper, turned to the sports page.

"Child's had too much already," Reenie said.

Gert looked at Jimmy. He didn't seem to be reading anything. But he wouldn't take his eyes off the page. His silent stare separated him from Reenie and Gert. How did he feel? How would any child feel? Like an orphan? Sure, he had Molly and Reenie and Gert, but his father died yesterday. And the circumstances were so strange, the boy had to feel abandoned.

Gert sat at the kitchen table and sipped her coffee. She couldn't find any words she wanted to say.

When Jimmy talked again, it was as if he were talking to a hole in the table.

"Are they going to tell you who did it?" he asked.

Gert glanced at his grandmother. Neither woman said anything.

"Are the cops going to tell who murdered him?" Jimmy asked again.

Gert was still surprised. She didn't know anybody had said the word "murder" to the boy. No one should have. They certainly weren't sure what happened. For all she knew, the police might have changed their minds, might have found the gun under the bed after all, might be calling it suicide again.

"Someone tell you that?" Gert asked Jimmy.

"On the phone this morning," Reenie answered. "The officer said it was 'homicide.'"

"I don't think he should talk to them anymore," Gert said. "Can you keep him here in the kitchen?"

"I can talk about it," the boy said. He turned the page once more. "I can do it."

"I know you can," Gert said. There is always a time a person needs to talk. Nine year olds are no different. She knew that. She just didn't think he should have to. Although she had plenty of questions for him herself. What did he know? What did he see? Did she dare ask if he saw a murderer? No. Don't be that specific. Leave it open. Let him supply the words.

"Jimmy," she said, "do you want to talk about it?"

"I didn't go upstairs," he said. "I left my books in the house after school and went outside. Grandpa was driving by."

"Grandpa?"

"Joe's father," Reenie added.

"What is he, ninety?"

"Close to it."

"He still drives?"

"Fit as a fiddle."

"He gave me a ride to David's, that's all."

"Jimmy, did Grandpa go inside?" Gert asked.

"No. He was driving by. That's all."

"Was your dad home?"

"I don't know. I didn't go upstairs."

"Did you see his car?"

Gert knew she was pushing the boy, but finding out about Joe's father added a new dimension. Another witness. Another bystander. Another helpless loved one. An awful lot of people for a murderer to rush past unnoticed. One more reason to believe it was suicide.

"Whose car?" Jimmy said.

"Your dad's."

"His car was in the driveway. But I didn't go upstairs. Grandpa gave me a ride to David's, that's all."

The boy had been glued to his newspaper all the while he told his story. He didn't look at Gert at all. Reenie was right — it was too much for him. A few details. Tiny scraps of information saved from the afternoon of his father's death. Repeated. Like a child's song. Over and over again. A round. He could talk to the police. He didn't go upstairs. That's all. He could talk. His grandpa gave him a ride to David's, that's all. He could talk to anyone. The car was in the driveway, but he didn't go upstairs, that's all. Gert touched the boy's shoulder and he crouched further into the newspaper. She pulled her fingers away quickly, picked up her coffee, took it to the living room. That's where she wanted to wait for the police. She didn't like them talking to the child like that, on the phone. Now the boy was withdrawing, flinching at the slightest human touch. God knows what that Cook fellow would come up with next. She wouldn't let him talk to the boy again, not if she could help it. But what about Molly? That was another story. There was no way to keep Molly from doing what she thought was right. And then there was Grandpa, Joe's dad, close to ninety years old. Couldn't have been involved. Gert sat down in a tall winged-back chair. She faced the window and watched for the lieutenant.

Reenie's voice came from the dining room, behind Gert, "Odd woman. Writes about Molly every day, she's got another one this morning..."

"Hmm?"

"In the newspaper. Jimmy's reading it now. Do you want me to bring it to you?"

"What is it?" Gert turn around.

"A gossip column of sorts."

"Should I read it? I mean, before they come?"

"They spelled her name right," Reenie said. "Molly's father always said it doesn't matter what they say as long as they spell your name right."

"Will it wait until they're gone?" Gert asked.

"Of course, dear. I don't get her drift today anyway..."

Gert could hear Reenie go back to the kitchen. Molly was sure famous. More famous than Gert ever dreamed. This was turning into some kind of carnival. She should have called a lawyer for Molly. Maybe she should call one now. Stop it, all of it. The police were on their way and Molly didn't even know anything about Jimmy and his grandfather. Didn't have the vaguest idea the cops suspected her of murder. She should know that before she talked to the police. They needed more time, Gert and Molly, but they weren't going to get it. From her chair, Gert could see Lieutenant Cook and another man — younger, heavier — get out of a car. They walked toward the house. The two men stepped onto the porch and stamped their feet, shaking snow off their shoes. Molly's mother answered the door. Gert went out to join her in the front hall.

"Did you find the weapon?" Gert asked.

"We'd like to talk to your daughter, Mrs. Stuart," the lieutenant said. "We need someone, and I'm afraid she's the only one..."

"The only what?" Gert asked.

"The first one," said the other man, "to find the body."

"Or the last one," the lieutenant added, "to see him before he died."

"She and the boy," said the second one. "And I already talked to the boy."

So it was the sergeant who talked to Jimmy. Knew about Grandpa, then. Unless Jimmy had left him out of the conversation.

Not likely, though. Jimmy was telling a story that never varied. The one he told Gert was sure to be the same one he told the sergeant.

"Sergeant Wertz," the stocky one introduced himself to Molly's mother.

"I'll go wake Molly," Reenie said. She turned around and went up the stairs.

Gert led the two men into the living room. Seated them on the couch, straight across from the winged chair where she had been sitting. They weren't answering her question about the gun. And what was it that firearms expert called it? The backsplash? In the sink. They wouldn't tell her if they found anything in the sink either.

"Ms. Peterson," he said, I think it's time for us to talk to the judge's widow." The lieutenant was as haughty as he'd been the night before. And as carefully groomed. He pulled back the sleeve of his sportscoat to look at his watch. His shirt had imitation French cuffs, the kind that can either be buttoned or fastened with gold links. He chose links, stamped with the emblem of someone's family. The sergeant was wearing a similar wool jacket, tweed, like the lieutenant's, but coarser and cheaper. And he seemed to have gained weight since it was purchased. Gert thought this second policeman's attitude was as similar to the lieutenant's as his jacket was. Cold-blooded, marblehearted. She already knew that from the way he dealt with Jimmy — just like Cook, but less polished.

Molly's mother came into the room with the tray. On it were blue cups and saucers, and coffee in a flowered china pot.

A creamer and sugarbowl matched the coffee pot. And so did the plate that held slices of banana bread. "Please," she said, "help yourself. I'm not sure how long it will take my daughter. She is still not well."

"She shouldn't come downstairs," Gert said.

"They're only trying to do their job." It was Molly's voice.

She had come up behind Gert, and she looked good, walking into the room in the morning light. Like a different person. Alert. Eyes wide open. Color in her cheeks. Black hair glistening.

Gert wanted to jump up and give her a big hug, but the lieutenant's cold gaze reminded her to be formal. She stood and reached for Molly's hand. Even without shoes, Gert was a head taller than Molly.

"Are you all right?" She spoke softly, as though Molly were a fragile, temperamental ballerina about to go on stage.

"Yes," Molly whispered back.

Molly looked good, but her voice was still as thin as blown glass. Frail enough to make Gert ignore the lieutenant's icy formality. She bent over and gave Molly a hug. Then she watched her friend shake hands with the two policemen, pour herself a cup of coffee, and sit down in the dark green overstuffed chair next to the fireplace. Molly had lived through her hour of lead. That's what Emily Dickinson would have called her trance the night before. But after her numbness, Molly may have been more breakable than before.

"First — Chill — then Stupor — then letting go — " The image of a ballerina stayed with Gert, this time a tiny porcelain one. Spinning around. Twirling on a pink satin platform when the jewelry box was opened and the music began.

The lieutenant started slowly, introducing the sergeant, reminding him of Molly's work as a prosecutor, trading anecdotes with the other man about what he called the Kiddy Sex Ring investigation. "Tinker Toy," the sergeant said they called it downtown. Molly did not let go. She responded calmly, as though she were interested in what they had to say about her work. She was one of them. A prosecutor having coffee with cops. Molly's demeanor had the same smooth presence her mother had carried into the room with coffee and banana bread. Gert supposed that's where it came from, the nonchalance. It ran in the family. Father and mother taught Molly stage presence. Aplomb at an early age. Molly always had it, even as a kid. The night before, it had been devastatingly absent. But it was back now. Gert hoped it would last.

"I was not sure you understood what happened yesterday." Cook paused at the end of his statement to take a sip of coffee. He was using the pause as a question. To make Molly talk.

"I know what happened," Molly answered.

She was untroubled, calm and direct. Surprised Cook, Gert supposed. Brief too. Molly responses were short and to the point. The lieutenant had wanted her to say more. He tried again.

"Did Ms. Peterson tell you?"

"No one told me. This morning, when I woke up, I knew."

"It must have been a shock, realizing what happened, I mean," Cook said.

"Strangely enough, it wasn't." Molly went to the table and poured herself another cup of coffee. "I thought when you realized something like this there'd be a loud scream, deep inside, but there wasn't." She went back to the chair. "It was more like someone whispered it to me. I guess it's because he did it himself, because it's what he wanted."

Sergeant Wertz leaned forward, "We're not so sure of that, ma'am," he said.

Molly looked from Wertz to Gert and back to Lieutenant Cook. For a moment, Gert thought she saw fear flash across Molly's eyes. Then it disappeared. If it had been there, Molly had controlled it. Tamed it. Tucked it away.

"What is it that you're not sure of, Sergeant?" Molly asked. Gert was amazed that Molly could muster a clear, strong voice.

"We're not convinced that your husband took his own life ..." Cook let his statement dangle again.

"You don't think ..."

"Looks like homicide to us," Sergeant Wertz blurted out.

Molly looked away, into the fireplace. Gert was ready to grab the two cops by the shirt collars and throw them out of the house. First they were friendly, trying to catch Molly off guard. And Molly was doing so well. So steady, unruffled. But that jerk of a sergeant. Any minute now he was going to start insinuating about the weapon. This was the same man who had quizzed Jimmy on the phone. Gert had been right not to like him. He was less palatable than the lieutenant. And she didn't care for the lieutenant either, sliding sideways into a homicide allegation when he called it a "fucking murder" last night. One second more of silence and Gert would have told the policemen to leave.

"I don't have any doubt that my husband took control of his own life and death," Molly said.

"Then, perhaps, when you found him he had a weapon in his hand?" Cook asked.

Molly looked at Gert. It was obvious she didn't remember.

"It's been ruled a homicide," Cook said. He poured coffee into his cup, added cream.

Gert couldn't watch any longer. "I don't know what more you plan here, Lieutenant, but I think it's time for you to leave."

"No," Molly said. "No, I want to hear more. What are you saying, murder? That somebody went into the house and murdered him?"

"That's exactly what we're saying. Somebody who could get close enough to shoot him in the temple. Without a struggle."

Gert leaned back in her chair. She had underestimated Molly. Molly was able to talk about it. Handling it well, too. The entire interview with the police. She'd forgotten how strong Molly could be. Molly had told Gert a couple years ago about her life, about it being divided into compartments, scattered in pieces, she said. And she had to live in those segments, live fully in each part, as though each fragment were a whole.

A piece of her at the courthouse. A piece at home.

Gert finally understood what Molly meant. She could see Molly call up her courthouse fragment now. The courthouse piece. She was treating this discussion of Joe's death as though it were work. The prosecutor had taken over. And Molly began to question the police. What had they found in the room? Nothing? What calibre gun had been used? They didn't know yet. She learned they had talked to Jimmy. Learned Joe's father had driven by but had not gone inside. Have you talked to him? Yes. They had. He had given Jimmy a ride, that's all. On his way home from the doctor's office, that's all. He didn't go inside.

It was ten minutes before the police took control again.

"We need to know a few more things from you," Lieutenant Cook said.

"Of course." Molly did not seem worried. She had encircled herself in her profession. The technique gave off an aura of strength.

Cook reached into the right pocket of his sportjacket and pulled out several sheets of blue paper, folded in half and then folded again. He set the papers on the coffee table. Because of the folds, they seemed to perch there, open, like a small book. It was Molly's handwriting all right. Gert wished she could read the writing from the across the room.

"That's mine," Molly hopped up from the chair, crossed over to the table and took the pages. Back in her chair, she opened the blue pages and held them in the light that poured through the window. She leaned into the words and read slowly, until her own pale skin seemed to take on a blue cast from the paper in her lap. Her lower lip quivered. Then she creased the papers shut and held them tightly in her left hand.

"Person who wrote that was scared or nuts," Wertz said. He was pointing a piece of banana bread at Molly when he said the words. The bread cracked in the middle, broke and plopped into his coffee. He didn't mind. He rubbed his hands over his cup to get rid of the last few crumbs. "Whoever wrote that note thought they were going to be killed," he said.

"It's mine," Molly said. She opened the pages and stared at the words again. "I wrote it, to you, Gert," she said. "But I didn't mail it."

Gert was on her feet heading toward Molly. But Cook made it across the room faster, in only two steps. He took the papers away from Molly and opened them.

"There's talk in here about devils and flames and evil. Stuff about human sacrifice. This your handwriting?" he asked Molly.

She nodded that it was.

"Reason I ask is that it has an interesting conclusion to it. Not signed or anything. But it's like a strange sort of insurance policy. Something you leave around if you're afraid someone very close to you is about to get away with murder."

He went back and sat down on the couch next to the sergeant. "I'll read from the last page: '... I am afraid. Everything is threatened. Work, life, soul. All in danger. If I die, it is no accident. I am afraid for my life. To think the person I love would want to destroy me ...' "

Gert looked at the two policemen on the couch. One spooning crumbs out of his coffee. The other holding the most private of Molly's thoughts in his fist. Enough was enough. She looked at Molly shivering, fighting back emotion. If Molly's composure had come from the illusion that she was an attorney rather than a bereaved wife, the fantasy was fading now. The portion of her life where she functioned as a successful career women was melting into the fragment where she had been a threatened, frightened wife. Words scratched on a handful of blue paper had sapped Molly's power to keep the segments apart. And when Molly was faced with all the pieces, she ended up on the edge of disintegration again.

"It's time for you gentlemen to leave," Gert said.

Cook ignored her. "You are sure it was you who wrote this letter?" he asked Molly.

"If you let me see the handwriting, I'll identify it," Gert said, "and you can leave."

"It's evidence," he said. "I can't be handing it around. We'll have it analyzed."

"Are they accusing me of murder?" Molly asked Gert.

"I think you should come downtown with us, answer a few questions, talk where there's no interruptions."

"Do you have a warrant?" Gert asked. "Some sort of order for her to go with you?"

"Not at all," Cook said. "I didn't think that would be necessary, not with an officer of the court."

"It is necessary," Gert said. "No exceptions. Didn't you say the same thing last night? In fact, it's going to be necessary before you do any more talking at all. Downtown, here, anywhere."

"It's obviously my writing," Molly was crying, talking at the same time. "It's not Joe's. I was frightened. I wrote the note. I guess I can't deny that. It's certainly not something he wrote accusing me ..."

"Don't speak to them anymore," Gert said. She went to the closet for their things.

"Not getting along well, then, you and the judge?" The sergeant was still pushing. "What, were the two of you having marital problems?"

"That's enough," Gert was standing in the middle of the living room with their overcoats. "You're going to leave now."

The lieutenant smiled as he looked at Gert's bare feet. "You're not in clerical garb today, Ms. Peterson."

"Please," Gert said, "remember not to come back again without a warrant or a subpoena."

"Like a caged animal. Backed into a corner. That's what the person who wrote this was acting like," the lieutenant put the folded stationery into his overcoat pocket.

Gert's only goal was to get the two men out of the living room. She pointed to the door. She moved between them and Molly. She took a few steps in their direction. Finally, the sheer force of her determination made them leave.

"You're describing a victim," she said to them as she let them out. "Not a killer."

"Not that much difference," the sergeant said.

"I'm surprised," the lieutenant looked at Gert. He took two steps backward across the porch. "Ms. Peterson," he said, "haven't you ever seen a caged animal pounce?"

CREED

Gert sat down on the couch and tried to be still, like she had been the day before in the airport. She wanted to stay out of Molly's way. Hoped Molly would put things in context, now the police were gone, by talking to her mother, talking to Jimmy, talking on the phone. Let her repeat Lieutenant Cook's outrageous comments. Let her replay the wild events.

Molly needed to settle her mind, retrieve her fragment of calm, regain the power she had before the police showed her the letter. Isn't that what this woman was saying in the newspaper? Sandra Gens. Reenie didn't like her. "Trying too hard to impress us with what she knows," Reenie said. "Wears her schooling on her sleeve."

"Does she think I've gone mad?" Molly was looking at Jimmy.

Jimmy shrugged. He turned and looked out the dining room window. "She's on your side, " he said. Gert wasn't sure the Gens woman was taking sides. But she did have a point. Molly needed time. No use Gert quizzing her now. If she waited — gave her an hour, maybe, that's all — then she and Molly could get to the bottom of it. Gert was sure. Patience. A little more patience. She folded the newspaper and set it down on the coffee table in front of the couch. She looked at her watch. It was ten minutes to eleven. At ll:45, she would talk to Molly.

Out of a large cloth purse Gert took her favorite books, one by Eliot, one by Newman. She opened the *Apologia*. It was always with her. She read it when she could, re-read it often, ever since she turned Anglican. Searching for answers, she supposed, seeking parallels, trying to find reason for leaving one church and going to another. She was like Newman — willing to believe, but needing to question. So much like Newman. But just the opposite in the end.

Read him backwards, she told herself. That's what she ought to do. But she couldn't read him any way, forward or backward. She couldn't keep her mind on his writings at all. Not today. Today's theological questions had to do with Sandra Gens' heroes and gods. Her pantheon of public figures. And Molly. Why didn't

Molly mail that strange letter about devils and evil and sacrifice? Why did she end up asking Gert to come and say Mass? And most of all, how did Joe die? Not Newman. Her mind wouldn't absorb Newman today.

She put her book back in the maroon fabric sack. It was 11:15. She picked up the other book. Eliot's *Collected Poems.* Her mantra. That's how she used it, over and over. Same as the rosary, she supposed. "You say I am repeating something I have said before." Dear sweet poet. She read more, "I shall say it again. Shall I say it again?" But the words did not sooth her. Eliot's poetry only reminded her. "And what you do not know is the only thing you know." She closed the book, shut her eyes, sunk back into the soft pillows of the couch and listened.

Molly was on the phone with the Wallblom fellow. So that's who he was, the man who loaned her the Datsun. He was from her office. That was apparent. Another lawyer. A woman was mentioned, someone he was with — living with or staying with — thank God. Gert had no doubt Molly was innocent, but it was good to know they weren't going to have to fight about a love motive with Lieutenant Cook. From the comments Molly was making, Gert thought Wallblom must be suggesting she keep his car for the weekend. Molly said she couldn't.

"If the two of you could come get it," she heard Molly say, "it would be best."

There was silence for a moment and Gert thought perhaps Molly hung up without saying goodbye, but then she spoke again.

"I am really very tired. Yes. A nap. You're right. In fact, I am about to do that."

"Should I take it to him?" Gert asked when Molly set the receiver down.

"No need. He's coming over today or tomorrow," Molly answered, then she went to the foot of the stairs and paused. "Gert," she said, "I am sorry, but would you excuse me a while?"

"Molly, I have to talk to you. Soon."

"I'm afraid I need a rest," Molly said.

Gert would rather have brought Molly coffee or brandy or whatever it took to jar her awake. There were too many unanswered questions. It was as though whatever was happening to Molly had been orchestrated long ago. As though Molly was involved in a drama that had been written and rehearsed over and over again, and now was simply unfolding on the stage.

Progressing, inexplicably, according to a formula that was beyond Gert's control. Yet Gert was part of it too. Repeating something she had said before. Reenie stood at the dining room table. "Should I run a bath, Molly?"

A faint smile crossed Molly's face. "I'm fine, honest," she said to her mother. Then she looked at Gert, "I'll go sort things out. I'm just not sure what I should do."

"Put everything in God's hands," Reenie said. "Say a prayer. It's the best thing to do."

Gert gave up. She told Molly to go ahead. Take a nap.

But it was time for Gert to stop sitting still. She couldn't stand being cooped up any longer. She had to get out. Trudge through snow. Suck in cold air. She had to search for answers on her own. Out there. The answers had to be out there.

Within twenty minutes, Gert had rented a car from a place called "Hire-a-Heap." They came to the house and picked her up. Right out to the house. None of the others would do that, not even the one that charged twice as much. She ended up with a dark brown Chevrolet, a '77, rusted, but it had what Gert needed — an engine that worked and a little heat besides. She dropped the driver off at the rental company and drove away, her tires spinning in the ice and snow. Never could figure out how St. Paul budgeted for plowing its streets. Sometimes it seemed the city didn't know the snow was going to come. At the airport, they knew, runways were as clear in January as in July. But there, in the city, plows were always a day or two behind.

Gert turned at the end of the bridge and headed up the hill toward Molly and Joe's.

In front of the house, snow had turned to slush. Gert's old rental car bumped down, into a mushy pothole, and then up again as she pulled into the driveway. All the way back, by the kitchen door, where she'd gone in the night before.

When she got out of her car, she saw the trouble. The house had ribbon all around it. Yellow plastic ribbon with bold black letters that spelled the words, "Do Not Cross — Crime Scene — Do Not Cross." Gert stepped out of the car. The ribbon blew in the wind and made a tapping sound when it fluttered against the railing at the back door.

"Damn," Gert said and pounded the railing with her fist.

There had to be a way to see something without breaking the seal. A window, maybe. More than one. She noticed several in

91

the kitchen, and a couple more along the side. But when she peered into the kitchen, there was nothing new there. In fact, her coffee cup was still on the table where she left it the night before. She walked along the side of the house by the driveway and looked into the windows there. One provided a view of an empty dining room. Another, a glance of the staircase and front hall. Sun bounced off the window. Glaring sun. It made Gert imagine she saw a figure inside. A shadow? More like a small person. Coming down the stairs. Disappearing again.

She ran around to the kitchen trying to follow the form. It seemed to have gone that way. Maybe someone was coming out the back. But the yellow ribbon was unbroken. She looked into the window, the kitchen was as empty as before. And she felt foolish, running through the snow, peeping in windows, seeing shadowy figures where none existed. She went back to her car and sat there, looking at the house.

It was a strange piece of real estate. Only neighbors lived on the driveway side. Across the street, in front, there was a park on the river bluff. And on the other side, around the corner, the yard just dropped off from under the house, a precipitous fall to the street. Wasn't there a retaining wall, holding it all up? Gert hadn't been around on that side for years. She backed down the driveway and pulled around the corner to look. From that point of view, the house was straight up. There was a wall, a rustic looking one, made of rocks and bricks and boulders. Built to look as though it had all been formed naturally. But too uniform, the repetition. A boulder, a rock, a brick. And near the back, there, straight down from the end of the house, was a shed. Not really a shed. A door. In the hill, or in the wall. Must be a storage room. For lawn mowers maybe. Or snow blowers. Or bikes.

Gert was about to pull over and park the car. Try the door to see what was in there. After all, there was no yellow ribbon sealing that. But the door swung out from the inside and a small old man looked up and down the street. It had been ten years since she'd seen him, but she knew him instantly. It was Joe's father.

He looked straight at Gert, and then, as though she were insignificant, he shut the door behind him and walked away. Where was his car? He must have parked it down the street. He kept walking.

Gert decided to go on ahead, to keep him in sight in the mirrors. That way he wouldn't know she was trailing him. She drove past the old man. One block. Two. There it was. Parked on the third block was a long black car. What was it?

Not a Cadillac. Gert was usually good at cars. A Lincoln. But bigger. Big enough for a limousine. She was sure it was his. He had a car like that when Molly and Joe were married. They all rode in it out to the country club for the bridal dinner. He could have afforded a chauffeur, but he didn't have one. Just himself. A tiny old man driving an enormously elongated sedan. That empty car had to be his. She turned into an alley and parked. In a few minutes, the old man inched through the snow and reached the black car. He took a long chain of keys out of his pocket, opened the door, and started the car.

Gert thought she did a good job, following without being seen. All the way across town. Funny. Such an old man to have a doctor so far away form his house. But that's not where he had been today. Today he was walking out of a hill. An elf. With a cane. Coming magically out of the ground.

Gert realized now she was following the old man home. East River Drive. The road along the Mississippi in that part of St. Paul was stunning. A dark, half-frozen waterway snaked its way through trees. And today, the branches were coated with frost. It was magnificent.

She stayed back, on the street, while Joe's father drove up the neatly plowed road that horse-shoed around the front of his mansion. Once he was inside, she left her car and walked up to the door. This house was a castle. No way to call it anything else. It had turrets at the roof line. Small arched windows with wrought iron bars. A balcony above the door.

Gert wondered where he got his money. Everybody wondered. Growing up in St. Paul, you knew this family. You knew the old man was rich. But you never knew where his money came from. Not from railroads, like the neighbors. Not from sandpaper and tape. Not from real estate or clothing lines or department stores or anything visible. Children like Gert and Molly who lived across the park from this castle had a guessing game about the old man. Was he a gangster or was he a prince? Gert drove her parents crazy with questions. Why was the old man rich?

"The crash," Gert's father used to say.

"Stocks?" Gert asked once.

"Brought his money with him, from Europe," that's what Gert's mother thought. "Austria."

"Russia. He's from Russia. Or the Ukraine."

"Same thing," her mother said.

"Not at all," Gert's father would argue. "It had to be the crash."

"If it were honest money, he wouldn't have to hide where it came from."

"What's so honest about the people who made money off the crash?"

Gert grew up believing something in between. Sometimes she imagined the family was related to the Czar. Or to Rasputin. Or both. Secret heir to Rasputin and the Queen. Living off bootie stolen by communists from the last Czar's ill-gotten treasury — then stolen back, wisely invested and, of course, pulled out of the market before the crash.

Gert still wondered. But the last time Gert asked about the family wealth was when Molly said she was going to marry Joe.

"He may be a judge, upstanding and all that, but nobody knows how his family got rich."

"Would you walk away from the man you loved because of the way his father earned a living?"

"I just thought maybe you knew ..."

"There are a lot of big families that did things like sell liquor during prohibition," Molly said to Gert. "But that's all over now."

After Molly married Joe, it didn't seem right to ask anymore. Bad manners to try to find out.

"Right place at the right time," that's all Joe used to say. "My father's always been in the right place at the right time."

And where was he now? Gert wondered if he was watching her. She hoped he wasn't. It was easier to talk to people who weren't expecting you. People you met accidentally on a walk. People you stopped to visit on a whim. They didn't have time to lock up their thoughts. They told you their secrets. And that's what she needed. Maybe she should have surprised him as he emerged from that cave. But it was too late now. She rang the bell.

"Who is it?" a scratchy voice came from a small square grill at the top of the door. It must have been a two-way system. She arched her neck so her voice would go straight into the speaker.

"It's me ... It's Gertrude ... Molly's friend ... I was at Joe and Molly's wedding ... Remember?" Her voice lilted up at the end of every word, as though each had question marks in it. As though the old man would answer, "Ah, yes, of course, Gertrude," and open the door.

Instead she felt something in her back. Poking her. It was round like the barrel of a gun. She was frightened. Without thinking of the consequences, she turned around. And there he was, the tiny old man, grinning at her, waving his cane. He poked her again with it, this time in the shoulder.

"Of course, I remember, heh, heh, heh," the old man seemed pleased to have tricked Gert. "It's a recording. Good idea, heh? Keeps people away when I don't want to see them. Crooks too. And bums. Keeps the bums away from my house."

He chuckled. A low chuckle. A lot like Joe's chuckle that night on the phone. Then he put his arm through Gert's, and led her toward a door on the side of the house. The old man stood only as high as Gert's chest, but Gert had no doubt she was being commandeered.

"We'll go inside this way, you see?" he said. "Then I don't have to turn off the electric lock on the front door. Did I startle you?" he chuckled again.

Once inside, Gert was shocked. Not by the opulence and grandeur she expected, but by the strange collection of furnishings crammed into the front two rooms of the house. There were several desks and file cabinets in what had obviously been meant to be a stately, vaulted-ceilinged living room. And next to it, where Gert expected a dining room table, was an old iron bed. And two televisions — one right on top of the other. There was a TV tray made out of pale green plastic or fiberglass. On top of it was a soiled aluminum plate, the kind frozen dinners come in.

"I don't use the rest of the house anymore," the old man said. "I don't have any need for more room than this."

He waved his cane toward the living room and motioned Gert toward a chair. "Take off your coat," he said and he walked around behind his desk and sat down.

Gert felt like an applicant for a secretarial job. If she'd hoped to surprise the old man into telling her why he was in that shed at Molly's house, she'd certainly lost the advantage. If anyone was surprised, it was her. Not the old man.

"Everything is going to be all right now," he said and he took out a cigarette. "Do you smoke?"

She didn't normally, but she reached across the desk and took the long black cigarette he offered her. "I think I will," she said.

He lit hers and his own and he inhaled, deeply. When he had blown white smoke into the air, he said, "Never have a cigarette

95

before the meal."

Gert cleared her throat.

"After," he said, "then it's all right. Look at me. I'm healthy. I only smoke after the meal. Did you have lunch?"

"Yes." Gert said, fibbing.

"Everything's fine then, with Molly and my grandson?"

"No. It's not," Gert said. "The police were there. Questioning Molly. She's very upset."

"Believe me," he said, "she'll be all right. And the boy too."

"I hope so," Gert said.

He only chuckled. He inhaled again, leaned back in his leather chair, enjoyed his cigarette.

"What if they arrest her?" Gert asked. She wanted to cut through his confidence. Frighten him if she had to.

"They won't," he said.

"They could arrest the boy," she said. "They have been talking to him too. The child. Your grandson."

He leaned forward and pointed his cigarette at Gert. This time he didn't chuckle. "We mustn't let them do that. You must promise not to let them do that."

She got through to him all right. He was furious. He crushed his cigarette in his silver ashtray and lit another.

"They tried to arrest me once too," he said, "but that was a long time ago. And it was in Russia. Are you telling me this is Russia? Are those police Cossacks? They want to arrest a small boy?"

"They are questioning him," Gert answered. "Someone killed his father."

"A boy would not kill. Only if someone harmed him. These police are as foolish as Russians. You know about the Russians?"

"Only a little," Gert said, remembering the elaborate history she had once assigned this man.

"A little is enough. They try to arrest boys. That's why my mother made me leave."

Could it have been a killing? Gert was putting scenes together in her mind again. Long ago in Russia. Yesterday in St. Paul. An old man murdered someone once — as a boy, someone who harmed him — and now he murders again. But when she looked at the tiny man on the other side of the desk, he looked helpless.

"Who knows? I don't know why she made me leave. There was commotion in the marketplace. There was a fight. I took a stick and whipped the legs of a horse. There was a man on the horse. He fell."

"Who was the man?"

"A man who had been cruel, that's all."

"What happened to him?"

He tapped a long grey ash from the end of his cigarette. "Maybe he was angry. Maybe he was after me then. My mother told me to run."

"Where?"

"Home. To bed. My mother sent me to bed and in the middle of the night she woke me up. She sewed ten dollars in my trousers while I was sleeping. She gave me my father's hat and his warm coat, and she told me to go. To walk, to keep walking until I found the people."

"And your father?"

The old man stood and walked across the room to a deep red lacquered cabinet in the corner. Gert hadn't noticed it before. He opened one of the doors. On the inner side there were paintings of angry swordsmen in medieval armour. Knights like St. George. Slaying dragons. He took out a bottle of cognac and walked back to the desk.

"My father I never heard of again."

"You tried?"

He shook his head.

"I mean later," Gert asked.

He exhaled and smiled. "Later, I was gone."

"Your mother?"

This time he shrugged — a small, slow lift of the shoulders.

No wonder nobody knew much about him. He had left everything behind, his parents, his homeland, even his will to remember.

"You found the people," Gert said. "You found them obviously. You must have walked for days."

"Days you didn't walk," he said. "Nights you walked. Days you hid in barns and cellars," he chuckled and he went back to the cabinet and removed two small glasses. He brought them back to the desk, set them down next to the cognac. Cordials. Two-piece cordials. They were narrow glass tubes resting in twisted brass vines, crystal in a cage.

"The boy will get away," he said as he poured liquor into one of the narrow glass tubes. "If these foolish policemen try to arrest my little boy, we will have to send the boy away."

This man was fascinating. Raising all sorts of possibilities.

Gert sipped her cognac.

He stood, and motioned her to stand too. He took out a ten dollar bill.

"You know what the ten dollars was for?" he asked.

"No," Gert answered.

"It was to show the customs man. To show that I was worthwhile. That I wasn't a bum. When they saw the money here in this country, they let me in."

Then, as though he wanted to take care of all the business before Gert settled back in her chair, the old man walked over to the coat tree, took Gert's coat down and handed it to her. She couldn't believe it. She was being dismissed. Already. And she was no closer to the truth than before she came.

"This way," he motioned toward the front door. Then he pushed three buttons, waited, pushed three more. There was a click. The old man went to the door and opened it.

Gert couldn't leave without answers. "You were in the shed at Joe and Molly's," she blurted out. "I saw you."

"He was a bum," the old man said.

"Who?" Gert asked.

"My son. He was a no good bum. That's all."

"You don't mean to say that," Gert said.

"He's my son. Don't worry. I'll say what I say. He never did anything. Not even as a boy. He didn't even know how to wash his hands. He didn't work a day in his life. He was a bum."

"He was a judge," Gert's head felt like it was full of sand. White sand. Heavy and light at the same time. The cognac on an empty stomach. The long black cigarette. The small man cursing his own son.

"I bought that for him. He didn't earn it. I paid for it. A lot. It was all arranged."

"How can you talk like that? He's dead. Tragically, dead."

"He's not dead. Bums like that are never dead. They come back. You'll see."

The old man's attack on his son had that same cold sound Joe's voice had on the phone when Gert called from Sweetgrass. "Haven't missed much," is what Joe had said about Jimmy. Now his father sounded the same. What was it?

"You should not have gone in there," Gert said. "There was a yellow band."

"No band on the cellar," Joe's father said. "You think I don't know about yellow ribbon? You think I don't know about cellars? You think I was born yesterday?"

"Cellar?" it hadn't occurred to Gert. It wasn't a door to a shed. It was an entrance to the basement, a way to get inside the house. And the small figure she'd seen fluttering inside when she looked in the window was not something she imagined. It was him. "That is a door to the cellar?"

"Young people know nothing," he motioned toward the door. "Good-bye. You are no different. You see me there, you follow me home, you smoke my cigarettes, you drink my brandy and you think I am a foolish old man who knows nothing."

He flipped his hand at her, as though he were saying "Scat." When she didn't respond, he flipped his hand again.

"Only the boy is different," he said. "He plays music for me. He reads to me. He's a good boy."

"He's my friend too," Gert said. "And so is his mother."

"Then help him instead of spying on me." He reached into his pants pocket again and this time he pulled out a sheaf of bills. He stuffed them into Gert's hand. "I have done what I can. If it is not enough, you give this to your Molly and tell her to take the boy and run."

"How much money is this?" Gert tried to count the bills quickly. They were fifties and hundreds. She was astounded.

"Enough," he said. "Enough to go somewhere. Like I did with my ten dollar bill."

"This is not ten dollars," Gert said.

"And this is not 1900 either," the old man said. "It takes more now to save a good boy."

The large door shut as Gert tried to hand the money back to the old man. She could hear buttons clicking on the other side. The old man reset the lock, turned on the tape recording of his voice. When she rang the bell again, the same scratchy voice she heard when she arrived said, "Who is it?"

Gert turned her back on the house and felt the money in her hand. She spun around and looked at the door and waved the fist full of bills and shouted one more time.

"Why are you willing to pay so much to get them out of here?" she demanded, but she expected no answer. She stood on the bottom step waiting to hear the scratchy recording ask her once again, "Who is it?"

Instead, the door opened and the old man stood there, leaning on his cane.

"Why?" Gert asked, almost in a whisper.

"Because," he whispered through the crack in the door, "because I know who shot my son." He turned and went back inside.

Gert ran down the driveway, hopped into her car, and headed once again for the West Side. The bills were stuffed into her coat pocket and she could feel the money swelling, bulging toward her soul. How easy it would be to use it, to trade justice for safety as the old man seemed to have done. Easy, proper, and maybe even necessary. The old man's voice echoed in her head, "take the boy and run ..." Run, like he had. Run. To escape the violence of a nation on horseback, a child had run. To escape the cossacks. But more. When the old man left his country, he had abandoned his own past as well. Father. Mother. Even the will to find or be found. All left behind. For the old man, escape was flight from more than geography. For him, escape was retreat from memory as well.

If he was the dark figure Gert saw flickering through the house, what was he doing in there?

"Everything I could," he'd said.

And what was that?

The only way to find out was to go in there herself. If he could get inside, so could she.

But she couldn't. And she knew it as soon as she saw the square brown house on the bluff.

Squad cars were parked on the street, at the edge of the park, everywhere. That fellow Martin from the night before was walking up the driveway. Once again, he was carrying his old black valise. She didn't want to attract attention, so rather than make a U-turn, she drove on, right past the house. She turned the corner and drove by the cellar door. It was open. A couple of policemen were standing there. One had a roll of wide yellow tape in his hand.

They had found the secret way in.

She drove on, down the Ohio hill, across the river, through downtown, back to Stuart's.

But things were no better there. A television van was parked in front of the house. People were pulling cables across the yard. A woman, a redhead, stopped a moment and talked to a cameraman, then she went inside the van. On the porch stairs, there was a tall, dark-haired man. Gert had a terrible feeling he was waiting for her. Must know what the old man did inside that house. Must know he claims he can solve the murder. Murder. Listen to what she was thinking.

She could see herself being dragged to a camera. She could imagine the reporter demanding an explanation for the money stuffed in her coat.

Drive through the alley, that's what she wanted to do, park out by the garage and steal in the back. Gert settled the Chevy into a snowy track and maneuvered it down the unplowed alley. But she stopped two garages away from Stuart's. There was another television van camped in the yard. She put the car in reverse, backed away, and went to the front again. There was no way to avoid them. She parked behind Wallblom's Datsun and walked toward the dark-haired man on the steps. As she drew closer, she could feel the money pulsating in her pocket.

But the reporter said nothing to her.

He was reading from a skinny notepad. Memorizing something. Rehearsing. Asking himself a question and answering it.

Reminded Gert of practicing for a catechism drill. She and Molly used to do it that way. Say both the question and the answer out loud. "Who is God?" Rote memorization. "God is the Supreme Being, infinitely perfect ..."

"Who is this woman?" the man asked himself. "This woman is a crusader, a savior of children, protector of victims, now suffering her own personal tragedy ..."

"Excuse me," Gert tried to open the door and nudged the reporter with the edge of the frame. "Excuse me. I can't open the door."

"You from the newspaper?" he asked.

He thought she was another reporter. Gert was relieved. "No," she said. "A friend. Please, could you move just a bit?"

"You're the preacher," he said. "Now I remember ... last night. We met last night."

"Not exactly," Gert said. "Could you move so I can open the door?"

He smiled. A wide smile. Gert knew the smile had worked for him, charmed people in the past. He moved, just enough for her to open the door, and asked, "Would you consider coming back out ... for an interview, a very short one?"

Gert shook her head and walked past him, onto the porch. No one followed. She was surprised how easy it was to get away. No one pulled her in front of a camera. No one demanded she explain why the old man wanted Jimmy to run away. But when she tried to open the front door, it was locked. She rang the bell and waited.

"Would you ask Ms. Stuart if she'd consider doing an interview?" the man tried one more time.

The door opened and Gert could see Molly standing in the dark hall. She turned to the man on the steps. "It's cold," she said. "I'm going inside."

CHORUS

Yellow second sheets, dry, faded, the older the better, Sandra liked to write on them. She pulled a piece out of the stack, still half-bundled in heavy grey wrapping, and rolled the page into her typewriter, up to where she could see the top of the empty sheet. She was the only one there who didn't compose straight onto the computer. Seemed like they took a chance that way; unfinished work ended up in the same electronic pile as finished work. That didn't seem tidy to Sandra. She liked it better this way — write it once on the typewriter, or three or four times — let yourself see the words on paper (faded yellow, the ink seemed to work better on faded yellow). Then once you're sure you've got an idea there, one that stands on its own, then go ahead and "stroke it in." Sandra didn't like the words that went along with computers either. She wasn't sure "stroking" had anything to do with writing. So she wrote first. On a typewriter. On faded yellow paper.

"What are you doing here on Saturday?" Steve, the re-write editor wanted to know. "Never saw you come in here on Saturday before ..."

"Too much going on with the Stuart thing," Sandra answered.

It was too much, a columnist trying to keep up with a breaking story. She shouldn't have promised to follow this thing, to interpret it. She should have let it go when the Judge died. She'd bitten off more than anyone with good taste ought to attempt to chew. Sandra pointed toward the three television sets perched on ledge about 10 feet from her desk. "They've been live for over an hour," she said. "I can't keep track of all of them at home."

"They're all saying the same thing," he said, "basically echoing your column. She's a hero. A crusader. A savior of children ..."

"Did I say that?"

Sandra was surprised the TV reporters were issuing praises. Hosannahs were not what she had expected this afternoon. She thought they'd be all over Molly Stuart like they were a few hours before. More inside sources from the coroner's office. Unsavory speculation about the Judge's autopsy results. And the hints of homicide. Where were the rumors this afternoon? And any minute now, she expected somebody to interview parents involved in the child abuse cases, or their lawyers at the very least. After all, the lawyers board had raised the question of Stuart's stability.

"You said even heroes have a right to crack up," Steve answered.

"All I said is we should give Stuart a break for a few hours," Sandra said. "Anybody get her on camera yet?"

"No sign of her," the editor answered.

"Maybe they're following my advice, " Sandra said. "Who do we have out there?"

"Kelly, and he misses you today ..." A voice came from one of the televisions on the wall, "... protector of victims, now suffering her own tragedy ..."

"They'll have her canonized soon," the editor said and went back to his desk.

Sandra began to type:

ST. PAUL, Minn. The Chorus by Sandra Gens

We used to play a game at birthday parties a long time ago. It went like this. We'd take a chair and put it in the middle of the living room. It was usually the fanciest dining room chair, the one with arms from the end of the table where your father sat, the one that looked like a throne. Then the person whose birthday it was would sit on the King's Chair and we'd circle all around. One by one each of us would try to guess something about the birthday person — something nobody else knew. Of course, her age was too easy, we had to guess something like her weight, or her middle name, how many cavities she had last time she went to the dentist, maybe even her highest or lowest grade. And it was okay to disagree. In fact, that was the object. For instance, if I said she had no cavities, the next girl could say she really had three. We went round and round this wheel, the guests forming spokes, the birthday girl at the hub, each of us shouting out our own point of view. In the end, after five or ten opinions had been ventured for every topic that was brought up, the birthday girl would tell the truth and the person who had most often been right won a prize. Sometimes it was fun. Some-times it was cruel. But the most interesting thing about that game was the person who sat in the throne. One honored subject. Only one. None of us accidentally sat in the place of honor. It was prescribed. We knew. It was the birthday girl.

And if she was offended by some of the comments, it didn't really matter; she got to open all the presents as soon as the game was done.

I thought of this game again today when I thought of Molly Stuart. You see, we've put her on the chair in the middle of the room. We've set her there and we're all trying to figure out why. So we're guessing things about her. Wildly throwing out ideas. At first, some called her a crusader. Then somebody else disagreed. Yesterday, somebody called her emotionally unfit and suggested she give up her job. But today again I'm hearing words like savior, and protector of unprotected ones. And now, after we've all had a day to consider the death of her husband, some of us have been calling her a victim of tragedy herself. We're all standing on the rim, tossing guesses at the girl in the king's chair at the hub of the wheel.

But are any of us right? And how does Molly Stuart feel about our guesses? She's not going to have a dozen gifts to help her forget the thoughtlessness we're throwing into her lap. And none of us is going to get a prize either. But we go on, guessing, disagreeing, guessing again ...

As Sandra typed, somewhere in the very back of her skull, behind the sound of the metal letters hitting faded yellow paper and phones ringing and voices talking in the newsroom and on the TV, she heard the editor calling her name. Sandra, Sandra, he was saying, Sandra, look at the TV. A squad car pulling up. A plain green sedan behind it, unmarked, another one. Two.

"Police are calling it homicide ..." came the male voice who had been talking out of the TV on the left.

"Kelly's just hung up," the editor was standing next to Sandra now, "he says his sources think the judge might have been killed by a kid."

"What kid?" Sandra asked. She left her chair and went over to stand in front of the television sets.

"No word," said the editor. "Kelly says no word yet."

Sandra looked at the television in the middle. A red-haired woman was standing in the Stuart's front yard. "We understand police are investigating several leads," she said, "and we understand that at least one of them is a child."

"Going over?"

"Columnists don't stake people out ..." Sandra said. She went back to her desk and picked up the phone. She reached for the white pages behind the dictionary on her desk. Columnists phone. They make appointments. Stuart. Hope it's listed. Stuart. What was the mother's name? Stuart. Here it is. Still listed under the mayor's — Stuart, Charles. She picked up the receiver again and pushed the numbers.

A voice, deep for a woman, said "Hello ..."

"This is Sandra Gens, I'm a columnist. I work for the "St. Paul Times"..."

"Yes," said the strong voice, "I've read your column. I read one a few hours ago."

"Is this Molly Stuart?" Sandra asked, although she knew it wasn't.

"No."

"May I speak with her?"

"I thought you wanted to let her have a few moments quiet, a day of rest, a little peace ..."

"I said that. You're right. That's exactly what I said." Sandra thought she knew who it was. The friend. The priest or minister who had guided Molly Stuart and her son to the cab the night before.

It wasn't going to be easy to get Stuart to the phone. "The facts seem to have changed. And I think she'd agree. I'd like to talk to her ... about the child..."

"The child?" If the voice knew anything, it wasn't giving anything away.

Sandra paused. She pulled the faded yellow paper from her typewriter. No matter what she learned in the next hour, this page was obsolete. She was glad she hadn't let it fall into that uncontrollable pile of copy in the computer. Homicide. So somebody was going to say the word again today. Murdered. By a child. What child? One of the kids in the investigation? Killing the judge? What on earth was the connection? Maybe it was too much to try to keep up. Hubris to try. But somehow she had to convince this woman to let her talk to Molly Stuart.

"About what happens to a child," Sandra said, spinning, not knowing where she was going, not willing to hang up.

"What happens when?"

"When a child is involved ..."

"When a child is hurt?" the voice said.

That was what Sandra needed. The slightest inference. The vaguest clue. Something to get her started. "If a child might have to fight back ..." Sandra said without finishing the sentence because she didn't know yet how the idea should end.

"I don't think it would help," said the voice.

"It might," said Sandra, "I think it might help the child."

"Are you here? Are you one of the people outside?"

"I'm downtown. In my newsroom. But I could come ..."

"I don't think it would be worth your while."

"Could you ask her?"

"What?"

"If she would speak to me?" Sandra tried one more time. "About the child. Tell her I think it might help the child."

"I'm afraid that's more than any prudent human should promise," the voice said, "Good bye." There was a click and a buzz in Sandra's ear. The priest had hung up the phone.

Sandra stuffed the page into her purse and grabbed her coat off the back of her chair. The prudent human. Give it the prudent human test. It was a test she often used to study the behavior of people in the news. Like she did the time the football player drove through a stop sign and injured a woman on a bike. Sandra drove out to that intersection to see how any prudent person would act under the same circumstances. And that time she agreed with the football player. When she drove down the street, she noticed the stop sign was hidden from view by a small oak tree. Conclusion, any prudent person, acting with normal care, might hit the woman on the bike. And now Sandra applied the test to herself. How would a prudent person behave? At any moment, one of those TV reporters was going to talk to Molly Stuart. She could feel it. It was time. Somebody was going to get Molly Stuart to talk. And she was going to be there, not as a voyeur or a cop, but as any prudent human being would be — especially a columnist bound by her own hubris-ridden pledge to follow this thing to the end.

CONSECRATION

"Second call from the writer woman, the one with the column, says she's coming over here now ..."

"Oh my God." Molly switched off the television and went to the bank of windows across the front of the living room. She lifted the edge of a sheer curtain — just enough to see out — then she let it fall back. She pulled the heavy green drapes shut, squeezing even the palest light of the winter afternoon out of the room. She was limp from the effort it took to seal it all out — cold air, police, reporters. All of it. "Gert," she said. "What do they want?"

Molly was exhausted. She had been trying to listen to everything — the people on TV, Gert on the phone. Now her legs were buckling under her. And her throat, it was swollen, and something was pounding in her ears, and her head was so heavy — she rested it against the dark green-draped window pane and closed her eyes. "Are they talking about Jimmy?"

"No," Gert was saying, "not really, just afterthoughts, they don't know what or who they're talking about ..."

What was Gert trying to do? Molly heard her, talking on the phone, about a child. It seemed everyone was asking about a child, on TV, the reporters, talking about homicide, saying police had a lead, to a child. And the police, they were back again, back talking to Jimmy again. Did they know something? Did Gert? Was Gert keeping it from her?

"Molly," Gert was asking, "Molly, you okay? I've got to talk to you."

"Gert, please don't try to protect me, don't hide what's going on, not now."

Gert looked puzzled.

"The reporter on the phone, the ones outside before, what were they telling you? Don't keep it from me, please ..."

"They have said that the police think someone murdered Joe, that they have a few leads, that one lead is a child ..."

"A child? What child?"

"They say they don't know. Molly, could it be one of the kids in your case? Is it possible?"

108

Molly was suddenly uncomfortable there, in the living room, so close to her father's experimental intercom; their voices must be drifting straight upstairs through the vacuum hose, up where her mother was keeping Jimmy away from it all, away from the phone and the door and the television. She pointed at the piece of screen, cut in the shape of a square and framed like a portrait hanging on the wall — Gert would understand the gesture, she knew about the intercom, no need to say "I don't want Jimmy to hear this" — Molly pointed and Gert nodded and the two women walked into the kitchen.

"Is it possible?" Gert asked again once they were there.

Molly answered "Yes," it was possible. She could breathe, perhaps, take air in, swallow it, get it past that spot she felt in her chest where everything seemed to be blocked; she'd be sad, but at least she'd be able to breathe if they were talking about one of the kids in her case. But she was afraid they weren't, and she didn't want to explain why. How was she going to tell Gert, tell her she thought everyone was asking about Jimmy?

It was as though Joe were back, laughing at her again; he'd done it, found a way to hurt them, found a way to keep her frightened. Still nagging at her, tugging at her was the feeling that Joe took his own life; he had control, he had the power, he made himself God — or Anti-God. Too long, it would take too long to explain everything: why she had smelled sulphur when Joe was in the house, why she had seen her picture going up in flames, why she had those dreams, dreams like the one she had that afternoon.

And Gert was asking so many questions. She was there in the kitchen, fumbling with her coat, fumbling with something in the pocket, questions, more questions. About Joe's dad? What? Did Jimmy talk to the police about Joe's dad again? Yes. And what? Did the old man hate Joe? Maybe. And why?

"I don't know," Molly answered. "It seemed he didn't know how to like him."

Molly went over to the part of the staircase that curved into the kitchen and sat down on the second step. She wrapped her hands around her knees, hugged them to her and then stretched and sat up straight again.

She wasn't answering well. What went on between Joe and his father was complicated: hatred had been passed from Joe's father to Joe — anger and vicious words echoed across the generations, and yet their lives were almost one life, their goals nearly always the same, outsiders would say they were close — and still they did not know how to love. Family trait?

More than that, isn't it? If a father hates a child, you figure twenty years later that child will hate his own children. Alienation repeated out of respect for parentage, cruelty emulated out of loyalty to imitation; maybe that's what happened, what made Joe unable to love his own son.

But Jimmy, not Jimmy, what would happen now to Jimmy?

"Can you trust Joe's father?" Gert asked.

"He's kind to me, kind to Jimmy," Molly said.

"Do you know why he left home as a boy?"

"No," she said. "Except it was a cruel place, a cruel country." Gert was asking question after question, and Molly couldn't answer any more. "No," she said again because her own mind was full of questions too. Not about the old man, not any more, she'd asked him a hundred times exactly why he left Russia, and he told her a different story every time; she had no more questions for him. No, Molly's questions were lodged deep inside and they didn't come loose easily. They were about dreams and waking, about the real and the imagined, about life and death and power and tyranny, about victims and sacrifices, about gods and anti-gods, about innocence and guilt and what differences there were among them. They were there, jutting out of a pile of thoughts in her mind, bristling up but stuck in a quagmire of confusion. So when Molly spoke again, they were not the questions she asked.

Instead she asked, "Have you eaten anything today?"

"No," Gert said. She had not.

Molly went to the refrigerator and took out a dozen eggs. She broke four in a bowl and began to whip them with a wire whisk. Cheese would be good, a cheese omelet, one for each, she could make them as people were hungry: now for herself and Gert, in a while for Jimmy and her mother. She set the bowl down on the counter and filled the basket of the percolator with dark brown coffee grounds, two, three scoops more than normal; Gert liked her coffee strong.

"What did you say, Molly?" Gert asked.

"What?" Molly had not realized some of her words had been out loud.

"Something about dreams, and being awake, and imagining."

"I may have said I dreamt about him again this afternoon."

"I wouldn't be surprised," Gert said. "What did you dream?"

Gert could be so calm, Molly had forgotten how easy it was to tell her things. Tell her anything; to Gert, you could say anything.

"It was about Joe. And about the animal head. Did I tell you about the animal head? The one Jimmy found at the front door?"

No, of course not, she hadn't told her, she hadn't seen Gert, hadn't sent a letter until last week, hadn't talked to her on the phone until the other night.

"Mol," Gert said, "there's a whole lot you haven't told me. What happened? What animal?"

"Joe says I talk about things no one wants to hear. Are you sure you want me to tell about it?"

"God yes," Gert said. "Especially now."

Molly was glad Gert had come. She was helping Molly unlodge memories, pull them out, wipe the mud away; remember, and talk — talk about the animal head, the deer's head, bleeding on the doorstep in the morning.

"It was one of those Sunday mornings, the kind Joe had when he'd been mad all weekend. He told Jimmy to go get the newspaper — woke him up, got him out of bed, told him to go downstairs and get the newspaper. When Jimmy opened the door, the deer's head was there."

"Poor kid," Gert said.

"Jimmy didn't say anything, put it in a bag, cleaned up the stairs, never said anything. It was Joe who was the angry one, he said it was one of the children in my case who did it — I never understood why he thought they would do that.

"But in my dream today it wasn't a deer head, it was an animal that kept changing from the head of a bull or ox to the face of a lion — roaring at the door, teeth bare, huge, bloody teeth, snarling, growling at the door. And suddenly it had the body of a bird, an eagle or hawk or a vulture, and it flew to my window and it kept on roaring, at the small opening at the bottom of the frame, growling and roaring, its mouth dripping blood and saliva. And you know what? I left the window open just a little because I was not afraid.

"And then, as though it were a bat, slithering under a door, through a small crack, getting inside, the animal head squeezed itself down and slithered through the tiny opening in my bedroom window. And when it came out on my side it was a tall man. A tall beautiful man with white hair, like Joe."

The percolator popped and hummed. Molly held a cup out to Gert and Gert filled it with coffee.

111

"He smiled," Molly said, "he was beautiful, his eyes twinkled — and I let him stay with me."

"Boy," Gert said. "No wonder. You don't look like you slept. I guess you really didn't."

"I haven't slept for years," Molly said. "Joe used to wake me up every couple hours, angry, always angry about something. Once he said Jimmy was coming in the room in the middle of the night — turning on the lights; once he said Jimmy was making strange noises outside our door. None of it ever happened, but in the morning he would punish Jimmy — make him get up early, early on Sundays. I think that's when he found that head, one of those days when Joe made him get up ..."

"I never saw you put sugar in your coffee before," Gert said.

"I never do. I thought I'd try ..." Molly stirred in another teaspoonful, "to see if it will wake me up. Gert, there's so much more."

"If I had only known," Gert said.

"Sometimes I think I knew," Molly said. "Like in the dream, sometimes I think I saw the snarling teeth but I ignored it because he was so beautiful. When he wasn't beautiful anymore, I thought it was my fault because it usually was. Usually it was me. I'm the one who made him mad."

"I would laugh," Gert said, "if you didn't look so frightened when you said that."

"He could be so good sometimes, so brilliant, so proper and correct in the law."

"Sometimes," Gert said.

Yes, only sometimes. Other times Molly thought he was something else, something the crazies talked about on Phil Donahue.

"Promise you won't tell anyone if I say this?" Molly asked.

"I promise," Gert vowed.

"Sometimes I thought he was the devil — when the animal head thing happened, I thought he did it, and I thought it meant he was the devil. I used to smell sulphur, in the bedroom, Gert, honest, I thought I smelled fire and brimstone, and that night, when I wrote that letter the lieutenant has, I smelled it again. I am afraid, Gert. I am still afraid."

Molly had to stop talking while she poured oil in the frying pan; when she thought of Joe, it was impossible for her to do the simplest things, no matter what, no matter how easy, she always

112

did it wrong. Like the oil now, a little too much in the pan. But she left it, maybe no one would notice, maybe the omelette would turn more easily, cook more quickly. She poured in the eggs and spooned cheese on top.

Gert was watching, listening, drinking coffee. Did she understand why Joe's death might be connected to the children in her case? No. She hadn't told her yet, had she, why it might be. But she knew she would, she was feeling more free, talking was easier, she wanted to tell Gert everything: tell her about Joe and the soap, about the boy and the picture, about the child whispering "sacrifice," about fantasies, fantasies Joe made her act out in bed.

A shiver ran from the tail of her spine to her neck. She may want to talk about it, but Joe didn't want her to. He didn't want her to tell anyone. Such power he had, such power he still had.

"You are insane," Joe's face appeared to her and he began to laugh.

Molly turned away. She cut the omelette in two, and with a spatula she slid half onto each plate.

"Do you think I know the difference between fantasy and reality?" she asked. It was important. It was the most important question she could ask.

Gert waited a moment before she answered. Then she said "Without a doubt."

"One minute I love him, the next I think he's the devil, and then I love him again," Molly breathed deeply. And then it came over her again, without her wanting it, without her asking for it, without her accepting the emotion. It was simply there, a kind of compassion, washing away her anger and fear, and turning every other feeling inside of her to forgiveness. She forgave Joe and she loved him again.

"I still love him," she said.

"He was more than lover to you, Molly," Gert said.

"He is my husband."

"He had, I mean he has, power. You talk like he's still alive. He's got a lot of power over you. He's got you swinging around in some sort of sun dance for him."

Molly knew Gert was right. Oh, yes. When the forgiveness came, it was hard to be disloyal; Molly was ready to push her memories back down again, to avoid telling what needed to be told. When the forgiveness came, it didn't matter that Joe was laughing. The dark love she carried for him could lull her back into secrecy.

113

"You think I'm dancing around the whole thing."

"I think you're dancing into it," Gert said, "offering yourself up to him."

"He used to make me do that, love him like that."

"Like what?" Gert asked. "Molly, like what?"

Could she tell? Yes, she had to. Molly sat down at the table. She unfolded a napkin and laid it across her lap.

"Joe had games," Molly said.

Gert said nothing.

"When we made love, he always had games. He'd make me pretend I was making love to his friends, make me call him by their names — that was awful. One time I said I wouldn't do it, and he said it proved I didn't love him and he refused to make love to me, for months after that, months and months, he wouldn't touch me; he called me a nymphomaniac, he told me to go to a sex clinic or get a man, get a woman, get some extra sex somewhere else. I was ashamed that my husband would abandon me like that."

Gert's silence encouraged Molly to keep talking — talk about it, talk about the scariest, the part she had been afraid to connect even for herself, what she had kept, hidden, deep in her memory.

"One day he said he wanted something special from me, proof I loved him, proof I wasn't trying to drive him away. He demanded a new marriage. He said he had an altar set up for a special ceremony."

"Why? Another ceremony, why?"

"This was a different sort of thing, Gert, he took me to a garage out on a road in the country and we looked in the window and there was an altar, such a strange altar, with satin ropes at each corner. 'Do you want to go in,' he said, 'and practice making love to me here on the altar of life?' "

"Did you?"

"I was starving for sex. I don't know, I was practically shaking. There I was, for months I had been living with a man, trying to love him, trying to make him happy, trying so hard — and all the while being ignored, and then this ... Can you understand? I needed him to love me."

Gert listened and nodded.

"But I couldn't. I cried. I refused. And he told me I had ruined his sex life, that I was trying to impose my standards on him; if I was a liberated woman I wouldn't have hang-ups. 'Go up to the bed!' I remember him shouting when we got home. 'Go up to the bed!' And I did. And he said if I were any kind of wife at least I'd pretend to be on an altar, sacrificing myself to him. And he tied me to the bed, hands, feet, and then he left the room. He said he'd know when I was ready and he'd come back."

Molly looked around the kitchen to make sure there was no one there except Gert and herself, then she talked again.

"I am so ashamed, Gert. I let him do it. He came back and said he was going to give me a new name, said he was going to call me Lee and he made me say I was named Lee. 'Do you love me?' he said. 'Yes,' I said. 'Then,' he said, 'what is your name?' And I said my name was Lee.

"But the end was worse. You see, inside his pretending was more pretending. At the end, he told me that he had played a trick on me — without my knowing it I had pretended to be someone else, someone named Lee , an actual person, who really existed.

"Then he said, 'What do you think of this? The person you let me tie to the altar, the person you pretended to be was really a little boy!'

"And he laughed. He laughed, Gert, because for him it was fun, for him everything was a joke, for him everything was inside-out."

Molly breathed deeply. She could see her own shoulders rising and falling, up and down, up and down.

"It was a long time ago," she said. "And I didn't seem to know what it was back then. I didn't know what to call it, except one of his jokes, one of his inside-out jokes. Of course, I shrieked and I cried, and he smiled about that too. He said I was crazy to even think twice about something that hadn't been real. And so I begged him to tell me for sure, tell me if there had ever been a child named Lee and all he said was 'You're crazy. You don't know reality from fantasy, red-blooded American fantasy."

Gert didn't ask any more questions. She didn't say, "How could you let that happen?" She didn't say "Shame on you for letting him do that to you."

Neither one of them said anything for a while.

Then it was Molly who broke the silence.

"Last year, the first child abuse case came up. And I began to hear stories — children telling stories about being tied up, about sexual rituals, on altars, in garages — and I knew what that was. I knew that wasn't fantasy. I knew that was real."

Gert wanted to hug her friend. Tell her things would get

better. But she also wanted to scream about Joe. Animal head. My god. Altar. Immolation. Be a boy. It was all too clear to Gert. Joe probably was abusing kids. Probably was connected to Molly's investigation. But she knew what Molly needed most right now was acceptance. Warm, peaceful and still. She sat there with Molly consuming the silence as though it were part of the meal. They drank coffee. They made toast. Toast from the oversized, elliptical loaf of bread that Irene Stuart brought from the bakery. Gert tried to fit a slice in the toaster but it was impossible. She went to the cabinet and took out a steak knife and cut the bread into two pieces, much more manageable shapes. Was it because they were women, she wondered, that they had mixed this talk of mystery with the preparation of a meal? Or was it simply because it had been the appointed time? Perhaps it didn't matter. She had been hungry. Hadn't had anything all day except coffee and cognac. And a long black cigarette from the old man who didn't know how to like his son. That's for sure. After what he said about him today. He still seemed to hate him. Bum, he called him, that was his eulogy for his dead son, call him a bum. Hatred did beget hatred, Gert was sure. Tyranny did beget tyranny.

But if it was so, then what on earth begat Molly's acceptance of it? That's what Gert wanted to know. Molly hadn't been raised that way. Her father, her mother, they'd never harmed anyone. Not Molly, Gert knew. Gert was there all the time as a child. The Stuart house was a wonderful place to be. No strong words. No anger. Not even much noise. Different from Gert's home, orderly, quiet. Not a training camp for boldness and anarchy like the nuns claimed Gert was raised in. Molly's bedroom smelled of sweet soapsuds. The kitchen floor was always polished, like it was right now, Gert looked down, high gloss on pale yellow linoleum. There was no dust in the living room. And dinner was always waiting. Roast beef. Onion gravy. Molly's mother ready to serve them all they wanted to eat. The mayor, talking about Aristotle and the need for a modern metaphysic. Molly joining in the talk. There was no fighting. There was no violence. Gert wanted to know who trained Molly to accept Joe's will as law? Not my will but thine be done. Who taught her to follow Joe along his tortuous paths?

Inside out. That's for sure. It was inside out.

Molly was playing out her own Divine Comedy. But she had become a backwards Beatrice — crawling behind her Dante. A Beatrice throwing herself at the feet of a companion who abased beauty and love. A Beatrice on her hands and knees, slipping further and further into hell. A Beatrice no longer able to lead, no longer able to guide, no longer able to express truth in the presence of this perversely beloved Dante.

Gert looked at her coat. She had draped it over her chair when she sat down in the kitchen. Of course, the money was still there. She would tell Molly about it as soon as they'd satisfied their appetites for silence.

It was five more minutes before Molly spoke.

"Never in my life have I tried so hard to please someone," she said.

"You made him God," Gert said. "The old white-haired one in grade school."

"God the father," Molly smiled. "Remember, the Baltimore Catechism. Why did God make me?"

To know him, to love him, to serve him in this world and be happy with him in the next. That's why God made me. "You tried pretty hard to please Him too," Gert said.

"The painting on the ceiling at St. Elizabeth's," Molly said, "Remember how scary it was?"

"God the abuser," Gert finally had it figured out. Fear God. Fear His righteous wrath. Who taught Molly to acquiesce to abuse? Not Molly's father, who was more professor than policeman. And not dear Reenie, unless silent witness to a battering God was a sin. Thy will be done. That's where Molly got her training. From God. And catechism, and martyr stories, and the nearness of sin. There was power in God's anger, and there was virtue in fearing Him. That's what rendered Molly a willing victim — running in the street in front of cars so she could please this God, wanting to die young so she could be with Him early.

"Molly, you, and Joe, that story about the altar, it's straight out of the Bible. Remember Abraham? Tying up the child and sacrificing him? Jesus, Molly, you married Yahweh."

Molly was laughing at that, but there were tears in her eyes. And Gert was suddenly sadder than she ever remembered being in her life.

It was clear. It was so. The God of their childhood was an abuser.

Bible stories ran through her head, babies slain and women stoned. Instructions that had to be obeyed, no matter what. What kind of God would order the murder of a child?

117

Yahweh.

Obey.

And look at the result. Even Molly who was trying so hard to save the victims. Strong, brave Molly, an obedient victim herself.

Weren't those the words the reporters were using about her? Strong? Brave? Crusader?

"The woman who writes the column wants to do an interview," Gert said.

"What about?" Molly asked.

"About the child ..."

"You said they don't even know who."

"About what could happen, when a child is hurt ..."

"I'm not sure what she means," Molly said.

But Gert thought Molly knew. Gert understood. She knew what could happen now that she had thought about it, now that she had seen someone trained for it, educated to tolerate it, baptized, catechized, degreed in the epistemology of victimization.

"Molly," Gert said quietly, "I think Joe abused kids."

"There's no proof ..."

"You didn't just tell me proof?"

"Words and jokes and fantasies. Wouldn't stand up in a court of law. Red-blooded American fantasy. Gotta know the difference."

"And Jimmy?" Gert asked.

"He never touched Jimmy," Molly said, but she looked worried.

"I don't think he had to," Gert whispered.

Molly stood. "I think we're going too far," she said. "It sounds as though you think Jimmy had something to do with this. Gert, is that what they're saying out there? When the news comes on again, is that what they're going to say?"

Gert took her coat off the back of the chair. She reached into the pocket, pulled the money out, and placed it on the table. "It's from Joe's father," Gert said.

"How did you get it?"

"He was in your house this morning. I saw him. I don't know what he was doing in there, but I followed him home and he said he knew who killed Joe. Then he gave me this. For you, and Jimmy, just in case."

Gert watched Molly pick up the money and count it. Was it Jimmy who killed his father? Patricide. The crime of kings. "A boy doesn't kill unless he's hurt," that's what the old man had said. And when Gert let those words slip to the Gens woman on the phone — "when a child is hurt" — that's what she wanted to know about too. What might happen if a child had to fight back. Self-defense. At the very worst. Gert had a sick feeling in the pit of her stomach. Ask Molly. Is there any chance? The thought turned metallic in her mouth.

"I'm going to talk to her, the writer," Molly said. She put the money in a deep pocket of her skirt. "She's trying to make it clear, child abuse, make people understand. I'm going to talk to her; don't you think I should?"

No. Of course not, Gert wanted to say. No. Take care of yourself for once. Take care of Jimmy. Go. Run. Get out of here before this twists us anymore. But she didn't say that. It might help, the writer had said on the phone. It might help the child. It might.

"What would you say?"

Molly's voice was soft, low. "Only the truth."

Gert could feel herself thinking her friend's thoughts the way she did that day when they were little, sitting on the edge of the street with the pitcher of dandelion wine. She could feel herself dreading the same awful truth, yet longing to say it, to hear it, to know it. Gert looked into Molly's eyes. Molly looked back. They seemed to give strength to one another. Awful, beautiful truth. Standing together, alone in the kitchen, Molly's words became Gert's and Gert's became Molly's. There was no difference. No difference between a butchered soul and an immolated body. Did Joe touch Jimmy? He didn't have to. Did God abandon Molly? He didn't have to. Did Abraham kill Isaac? He didn't have to. A person was torn. A human was sacrificed. And it was time to admit it, to say it, to give it a name.

If ever they had been able to read each other's minds, this was the moment. They left the kitchen and walked together toward the front door.

Elevation

Molly put on Jimmy's ski jacket, the one she'd worn last night after the police took her coat. It was skimpy under the arms, but it almost fit. Anyway, it didn't matter how it looked. It would have to do; she wanted to get outside, right away. She had decided there was only one way to save a child, whatever child, every child.

There, in the snow, they were all waiting. "Sandra Gens?"

When Molly called the name, they all came toward her, a dark-haired man, a red-headed woman, three men carrying TV cameras, a woman with a Nikon.

"Yes," said a woman. She had a beige fedora hat pulled over brown hair. She carried a slim notebook and a fountain pen and a purse, and she wanted to talk to Molly alone. "Perhaps we should go back inside."

But Molly had decided to talk to all of them, to send a message, to explain the horror of this and all violence, to hold an idea high, so high that no one could ignore it any more.

We've got to stop the sacrifice.

Before Molly could start, reporters began asking questions. The red-haired woman was talking about a child as a victim. Can a child respond? Will a child fight back? How?

Yes, Molly said, victims can respond. And yes, they may fight back. And yes, they might wait. And yes, they could catch the abuser unaware. And yes, they might plan. And yes, they might pounce. And yes, they would feel that retaliating against a sleeping person was self-defense.

The woman in beige, Sandra Gens, cleared her throat. "Self-defense? Planned, in advance, self-defense?"

"In a case of abuse, I'd call it self-defense."

"How would you, as prosecutor, react to such a case?" asked the dark-haired man.

"Quite honestly," Molly said. "I would not."

"But what about his case?" the man asked. "This tragic death. Your husband. Police tell us they suspect a child."

"Yes," Molly said. "A child."

And they all began to talk at once. And none of the questions was finished and all of them were started and why, a child, why? And a connection, was there a connection? And pardon, the thought, pardon. But the judge, had he, the judge? Be quiet, we can't hear, be quiet.

And Molly looked up and Wallblom was there, and so was Joe's father.

"Don't talk," Wallblom said. "I don't want you to talk."

But yes, Molly said, she would.

And microphones came toward Molly again and she took a deep breath and she spoke.

"Yes," she said, she believed a child had been hurt, and "Yes," she said, she believed her husband had done the hurting, and "Yes," she said, if a child struck back, she would call him innocent, and "No," she said, nothing more should be done.

"It is time to stop the sacrifice."

"Self-defense?" the red-headed woman asked.

That was the word.

"Proof?" the man wanted.

"Enough," she said, "enough."

Someone handed her an earpiece. "Put it on, could you, put it on." And now there were other voices coming into her ear. The producer, back in the studio, the anchor. Could she, please. Live on the air. Just talk to him.

"Soon?" she asked.

"Yes," said the producer.

Yes.

Now.

COMMUNION

Gert sat in the living room, watching reporters interview Molly on television. Before they were halfway through, she knew it was a mistake. Common sense should have dictated staying aloof from the press. But they had both been driven by some spirit, some inexorable force that made it seem reasonable for Molly to go outside to talk to Sandra Gens. Once there, it seemed reasonable to stand in front of cameras, talk to them all, spell out this outrageous truth. Outrageous. Great God almighty. When you said it on TV, it was outrageous. And Jimmy's jacket didn't help, hiked above her waist, pulled across her chest.

"Repeat it for our viewers, will you? And for me? To be sure we have it right," the red-haired woman was saying to Molly. "You believe some child may have been hurt by your husband — the judge — and that this child may have struck back in self-defense?"

Molly cleared her throat and nodded. "It would be possible."

"And you don't believe anything should be done about it?"

"No, I don't."

Molly smiled. It was that odd smile that came over her sometimes when she thought she had solved a problem. No, Molly. Frown. Grimace. Pout. Do anything else. Please. Anything but the smile. In person, it might be all right, but on television it looked like the smirk of a maniac.

Molly talked again. "We've got to stop this somewhere — violence has to stop; all of us, all adults have to begin admitting when we've harmed our children, and stop. It's very simple."

They switched back to the anchorman in the studio. "It would seem a legal stance that goes well beyond turning the other cheek."

"To be fair to everyone here," the redhead inserted her comment, "remember this is an immense shock." She seemed to be trying to protect Molly. "A dead husband ... hints a child is suspected ... a child of her own..."

Behind the redhead, Gert could see Sandra Gens. Her hat turned this way and that, as she glanced from the TV reporter to Molly, and from Molly to the TV reporter again.

Gens knew it was going badly too. Gert could tell.

The redhead went on, "...as prosecutor in this sex abuse case, she's become advocate for all children in the county ..."

"Well, all right, then," the anchor said, "ask the prosecutor for me, will you, what kind of prosecution is she supporting? Vigilanteeism? Giving kids permission to kill all the people they think have done them wrong?"

"Not at all," Molly's voice broke in before her face came on the screen. "These kids are scared. They've been threatened with everything imaginable, including human sacrifice. We have some sort of Satanic cult operating here in the city."

Gert went and sat right in front of the TV and turned up the volume. It was far from over. She should have held her back. Should have kept her inside.

The anchor said, "You accusing your own husband of sacrificing kids?"

"It's all the same," Molly said. "It doesn't matter."

"Could you explain that?" the woman in the hat seemed embarrassed that she'd interfered, spoken on television, out of turn, but she repeated her question again. "I'm sorry, but could you tell me what you mean by that?"

"Verbal ... mental ... you call it brainwashing when it's done to a prisoner of war; it's all the same because the effect is the same."

"Brainwashed kids?" the anchor asked. "Defending themselves by shooting first? I thought when somebody defended himself a little too early, like before, let me stress that word — before — the threat of bodily harm, I thought we called that murder in this society."

Molly's point was too subtle for television. It was a problem for an ethics seminar or a revelation for the confessional. A prayer for forgiveness. An entreaty at the last judgment. A cry for change from a morality that promised safety by imposing its own harm.

"What about your own son?" the anchor's voice said. "Was your son hurt? Is he the suspect?"

Gert could see that Molly didn't hear the last remark. There was a close-up of her, but she wasn't reacting. She had a vacant gaze on her face. She tapped at the plastic piece in her ear.

The redhead had to repeat the question for Molly. "Was your son Jimmy harmed?"

There was a pause. This time Molly heard, but she didn't answer. She turned away. She stared off into space. The reporter

123

waited. Finally, Molly looked back into the camera.

"Yes," she said. "That is possible."

"What's possible? Is she saying her son is the suspect?"

"No. I think what she's saying is that her son may have been harmed. Is that it?"

"Yes," Molly said yes.

"In what category would you place the abuse?" the redhead wanted specifics. "You've just been talking about verbal, physical, sexual ..."

"There are no categories," Molly answered. "All of it is the same; there is no difference; it doesn't make any difference."

The picture of the two women remained, but the anchor's voice came on again. "Amazing, absolutely amazing. Is she saying that a kid could kill somebody with impunity because somebody called the kid a name?"

No one answered.

"Well, I'm afraid we lost sound completely now," he said. "We'll certainly clear that up quickly because we'll be hearing more on this story, I'm sure." He continued to talk as the view of Molly and the crowd of reporters became more and more distant. "We're attempting to get additional comment from Country Attorney Eugene Blattner and from police, and when we do, we'll bring it to you. Hopefully, before the end of the newscast."

The view of Molly and the redhead and the dark-haired reporter and Sandra Gens had been widened now to include others, some with cameras, some with notebooks. It was hard for Gert to see, exactly. She knelt in front of the set and looked at the picture, small now, perched over the anchor's right shoulder. The shot revealed the sidewalk as it curved behind the crowd. And that's when Gert first noticed him, walking between the TV lights and the dusk. The familiar figure. The tiny silhouette. The small shadow. The old man, limping, but moving quickly through the snow. Gert stood and ran to the window to watch where he was going. Foolish to stay posed in front of the TV set when what she wanted to see was right outside. It took a moment for her to focus on him. There was a difference between the real view and the TV view. This was much messier. Crowded with people and lights and wires that didn't show on the television screen. And it was getting dark outside. But it was Joe's father all right. He walked behind Molly and paused. She turned and said something to him. He went on, pushing his cane into the snow, moving quickly across the icy walk, until he reached a squad car parked in front of the television van. What was he up to now? There. He stopped. He tapped on the window of the squad with his cane, and he waited. The window opened. Gert expected to see Cook or Wertz, but it wasn't either one. It was Martin, the firearms man from the night before. He stepped out and opened the back door for the old man. Once Joe's father was inside, Martin shut the back door and slid in behind the wheel again. The engine went on, but it must have been for warmth. The car didn't move. Windows were all shut. Frosted too. Gert couldn't hear or see a thing.

She opened the big oak door. She didn't know why. It wasn't going to do any good, but she stood there anyway. She saw Molly leave the group of reporters and come toward the house. There was a man with her, one Gert didn't know. He had sandy hair and freckles and he should have been fair, but his face had turned dark red, almost purple. They walked onto the porch.

"I'll get your keys," Molly said.

So it was Wallblom. When he spoke, Gert knew his odd flush was from anger.

"You're cracked, Molly," he said. "You let your husband push you till he made you sick, and now you've cracked, right there on television, you've gone absolutely out of your head, insane."

"Thank you for the car," Molly said.

"You know how you looked out there?"

"I know."

"What are you doing dressed like that? Whose jacket? The kid's? You look like you're on leave from an institution ..."

Molly looked straight at him. She said nothing.

"Look. The boss sent me over here to see if you're nuts or what. Cops showed him a crazy letter you wrote claiming Joe was the devil. Wasn't that bad enough? Now you go on TV and say it's okay for kids to go after their parents. ... Why? Because some mentally confused kid made some crazy claim about human sacrifice?"

"Every day I ask children to tell the truth," Molly said. "And that's all I did out there now. I tried to be an example."

"An example of idiocy," he said.

Molly brushed by Gert to the rack of keys hanging in the hall. Wallblom's Datsun keys were there, where Gert had hung them this morning. Molly went back to the porch and handed Wallblom the keys. He took them and left.

"Sorry I didn't introduce you, Gert," Molly said, "there didn't seem to be an opportunity, did there?" Molly hung Jimmy's jacket in the hall closet. "How did it look to you, on TV, how did I do?"

Gert didn't want to say. She opened her mouth to speak and she stuttered. Molly hadn't done well. It was obvious. People were going to agree with Wallblom. What had seemed so true and pure to the two women when they talked alone in the kitchen was not palatable in public. And the press knew it. That anchorman knew it. Before this thing was over, he was going to eat Molly alive. And some of the reporters would presume Molly staged the whole thing to protect her own son. Maybe that was Cook's plan all along. Maybe that's why he fed the stuff about a child suspect to the press. Maybe he wanted to scare Molly into doing something for Jimmy. Gert felt responsible. She as much as told Molly to go out and talk to the Gens woman. Some sort of Midas touch. Tried to pull Molly out of the fog, make her see clearly. In the end she propelled her into the vortex of live TV. Snap her out of it? Are you kidding. Now the entire city thought Molly Stuart was strange. What was the Gens woman going to write tomorrow?

"As bad as Wallblom said?" Molly asked.

"No, really," Gert said. "Not bad, not really." But pretending made her blush.

Molly looked at Gert and shrugged. She shook her head. "Gert ..." she started to say, but she didn't finish. She turned and walked away.

Gert recognized Molly's resignation. It was her next time stance — maybe next time she'd go all the way, maybe next time Gert would go along with her. Maybe the next time she ran in front of a car, everyone would understand. Next time. Still as dangerous as it had always been.

"What are you going to do now?" Gert asked.

"I'm going up to check on Jimmy." Molly smiled that smile again and she ran up the stairs to be with the little boy who seemed lately to be more and more alone. Sealed in, like his father. One room, like the old man.

"Did I see Joe's father out there?" Gert called after her.

"He was there," Molly stopped halfway up the stairs. "He didn't want to come in. He said he was waiting for the police."

"Mol," Gert said. "The police. Why do you think they're here again?"

"Don't know. Keep an eye on them for me, will you?"

126

Gert went back to the door and opened it. Cold air, spiked with snow, rushed over her face. She was blinded by lights flaring out from behind the cameras. The old man must still be in the car, she supposed, but she couldn't see anything out there but spotlights. She closed the door and turned around. Reenie was hurrying into the living room.

"Gert, come quickly," she said. "It's that lieutenant. Turn the channel. He's on the other station."

"Where's Molly?" Gert asked.

"Upstairs. She doesn't want Jimmy to watch. Hurry. Here. There he is. Listen."

It was Cook. Out there on the street. And Martin standing next to him. That's why lights were glaring. They were aimed at the police. Cook was wearing his overcoat, a stylish black and white tweed. But the wind had twisted his hair, and bathed in the garish prominence of live TV, he didn't look comfortable. He never glanced away from the page he was reading. He didn't pause to breathe. Not until he had to. Then he gasped.

"At approximately 12:47 p.m. today, an officer in the homicide division of the St. Paul Police Department received a phone call from an individual claiming to have information about a weapon involved in the death of a county district court judge. That individual gave a location where we could find that weapon and subsequently refused to identify himself, claiming to be at the place where the deceased had been found last evening. Said location having been roped off and marked as a homicide scene, officers were immediately dispatched to the site where the weapon was found."

So that's what the old man was doing in there. He was doing "everything he could" — leaving a gun. But how did he get the gun in the first place? Must have taken it the night before when he picked up Jimmy. The boy said his grandfather never went inside the house. Just gave him a ride, that's all. But Gert didn't believe it. She hadn't believed it since she saw the old man coming out the cellar door that afternoon. Police must have come right after they left. Missed them only by minutes. No more than minutes. Did they know it was Joe's dad who made the call?

"Ballistics tests show that the weapon is the one that was used to cause the death of the decedent. Forensic tests also show that blood on the weapon matches the blood of the victim."

Martin's backsplash. It was there on the gun.

"Since finding the weapon, we have spoken to the citizen who made the call at twelve forty seven and we are convinced that the witness acted in good faith and in accordance with his understanding of the law. We have no intention of pressing charges against that individual at this time.

"This statement will, we hope, put an end to rumors and allegations about human sacrifice. It should also end speculation that the judge was murdered by a child reacting to such threats. There is no such problem here in this county. Statements by the press that a child had been named a suspect in this case are totally unfounded. No such statement was made by me or anyone associated with this case. Medical examiner Dwayne Kraus has ruled the judge's death a suicide, as has been apparent from forensic evidence from the start. Thank you."

Cook breathed heavily into the microphone. Gert wanted to run outside and scream at him. What did he mean, apparent from the start? First he tried to make Molly look like a murderer, then he leaked the stuff about a child, and now he denied it. The only thing that was apparent was that he'd do anything to cover himself. Cook backed away from the lights, leaving Martin alone in front of the cameras.

"Who was the citizen who called?" said a reporter.

"Was it a man or a woman?" asked another.

"Why isn't this being investigated as homicide?" said a third.

Martin ignored the first two questions. "We have no doubt this is a suicide," he said. "The evidence is uncontrovertible. County Attorney Eugene Blattner has met with the medical examiner and with me. He is convinced — as are the rest of us — this case has never involved anything other than suicide. And now, the case is closed."

So quickly. They had changed it all so quickly.

"Are you aware that the judge's wife made a statement only moments ago that her husband may have abused or frightened a child into killing him?" It was the Gens woman.

"Yes," Martin said. "I'm very aware of that statement. It's why we're here now, in front of these cameras. Why Lieutenant Cook has shared the information we have with the public here tonight. In fact, the county attorney requested that we make this statement to clear the air."

"What's your reaction to her claim?" asked the dark-haired fellow.

128

Martin didn't answer. He looked around for Cook. Then he stared at the ground, or at his own shoes, until finally the lieutenant stepped back into the light. Cook coughed. He took out a handkerchief and dabbed at the corner of his eye. He sniffed as though he were holding back a sneeze. Then he looked up and spoke.

"I would simply recommend the lady take a very long rest."

"That's all." Martin waved his right hand at the lights. "Thank you. That is all."

The policemen turned their backs to the cameras. The picture flashed again to the anchorman in the studio. He spoke quickly. A tragic suicide, he called it, one which had apparently left the judge's wife, an assistant county prosecutor, on the verge of emotional catastrophe. The anchor promised more details at ten and then, abruptly, he signed off. It was six thirty. The news had ended. A game show came on.

"Thank God," Reenie said. "It's over." She took Gert's hand and squeezed it hard. "We must all thank God for seeing us through troubling times." Then she went to the television and turned it off.

When Reenie left the room, Gert snapped the TV back on. No sound, just picture. She sat on the floor, watching as the game show contestants competed in silence. She wanted to say "Thank God" too, just as Reenie had, but she couldn't. She was not relieved. To her, nothing felt like it was over.

LAST GOSPEL

After sitting in the yellow-grey light of the silent TV for an hour, Gert stood and shut it off. There'd be no more interruptions. There'd be no more news.

Molly had come down a while ago and told her it wasn't necessary to keep an eye on the TV. Not any more. The cameras were gone. The reporters were gone. Molly said everything was all right. Said she was going back upstairs to sleep. She could rest now that everyone was safe. Even Joe, she said. Even Joe was safe because he had done what he had always wanted — he had controlled life and death.

It was a curious thought that brought Molly peace. A strange idea that made her sleep.

Gert went into the kitchen, poured herself a cup of coffee and began to clean the dishes. Reenie didn't have a dishwasher. She thought they cost more than they were worth. Gert squeezed pink liquid soap into the dishpan and turned the water on — hot. A flowery scent steamed up from the sink. Funny, she expected it to smell different. The last twenty-four hours had been so extraordinary, she expected everything to change. She wouldn't have been surprised if colored light came out of the faucet instead of water or if perfumed soap suddenly had no scent at all. But the ordinary remained ordinary. Soap and hot water. It still smelled the same.

She heard the phone ring. One, two, three times. Someone answered it upstairs. Reenie, she supposed.

Gert rubbed the omelette pan with a steel scouring pad. Bits of eggs and cheese fell easily into the sink. She was glad Molly was resting tonight, because tomorrow they would have to decide what to do.

Calling it a suicide, saying it was all over, that was okay for tonight if it brought Molly sleep. But Gert didn't believe it for a minute. Not any more. She was convinced they were going to have to begin worrying all over again tomorrow. Gert held the pan under the faucet and ran hot water over it. If only she could clean away her doubt that easily. If only she could rinse away apprehension. If only she had Molly's peace.

But to Gert it seemed clear: today the old man had saved the boy from the police; tomorrow, Molly and Gert would have to find a way to save him from himself.

Hot water was pouring into the sink, and at first she thought the high-pitched squeal was coming from the faucet. It was a whistle, like the sound of water whining through pipes. Gert turned off the faucet, but the screech continued. It swelled into a moan, then to a scream, then to a wail that penetrated every room in the house.

Gert grabbed a towel. She tossed it back and forth in her hands to dry them. Then she dropped it on the floor and dashed up the short set of steps that led from the kitchen toward the large staircase in the hall.

There, standing on the landing, was Molly. She was wearing an old maroon robe that must have belonged to Joe or her dad. Her hair — shiny and smooth in the morning — was twisted and matted from her brief nap. She was sobbing and crying and calling, "No, no, no ..."

Her peace was gone.

Gert extended a hand. "Molly," she said, "I'll do anything I can to help." She presumed the worst had happened. The child must have confessed. The police must know. The old man's scheme must not have worked.

She put her arm around Molly's shoulder and was going to lead her down the stairs but Molly broke away and pushed past her. She ran through the kitchen, into the pantry, to the wall with the phone. She pulled the receiver from the hook and punched numbers wildly. Then she shouted into the phone, "No. You can't! You mustn't! People won't allow it."

"Must ... not ... what?" Gert asked.

"Mustn't send the children back."

"The children, Molly?"

"Mustn't close the case."

"Your case?"

"The county attorney and the attorney general and the governor, they've been meeting; they saw what I said on the news and they've closed it, Gert, they fired me, and they closed the case." Molly walked to the chair and sat down.

"Can they do that? Can't you appeal?"

"It will be too late. It's already too late. While I was sleeping they sent the children home."

"Molly ..."

"They say I'm crazy, Gert. They say what I said is crazy."

"Wallblom? Can't he handle it until you clear this up?"

"He's with them. He's on their side. He was with them when they called."

Molly who had tried to save the children. Molly who no longer could. Gert watched, helpless, as Molly began to weep. Deep, throaty sobs came from somewhere below her ribs and sent spasms of grief up her body as they climbed into her voice.

"It will happen again and again to every one of them," Molly sobbed. "Over and over again. It will never stop."

Gert felt powerless. There was nothing she could do to stem the continual sacrifice Molly was talking about. Nothing she could do to stop the slaughter of the innocents. Or of people, who, like Molly, try to protect them.

Gert poured a glass of sweet red wine for Molly and led her upstairs, to the sleeping porch, to the room Molly loved. She opened the window shades and lit a candle in the cyclone lamp Reenie kept on the lace-covered desk. The wax was scented. Sandalwood or Bayberry. The glass chimney back on the lamp, Gert went to the bathroom and rinsed a small cloth in cold water. She twisted it, ringing water into the sink, until it was only damp. Then she took the rag to Molly and put it on her forehead. She told her to close her eyes and sip her wine and let the cool rag pull away everything but calm.

Gert stayed with Molly, saying nothing. Contemplating the unpeaceful quiet that had proceeded Molly's defeat. Molly had been approaching this moment for years. Her marriages. Her politics. Her flirtation with all of God's tragedies, even as a child. Gert should have seen it last night. It should have been apparent. Molly, sitting there in a trance, not accepting, not believing Joe was dead. He had squirmed and pushed his way into her head until there was no more room for Molly herself. And today, Jimmy and the children. It was a transubstantiation of sorts. Molly, still appearing to be Molly, taking on the substance of those she loved. Becoming a savior, not as she would be, protector of the children. Not as she should be, prosecutor of the unjust.

But as she was and will continue to be, a victim herself.

Transubstantiation all right, but it was as though at the holiest of moments — instead of the bread becoming the sanctified body of Christ — Jesus had become the bread. Simple bread. Consumed. Gone.

Why hadn't she warned Molly?

"The children will never trust anyone again," Molly said. "They will never trust any of us again."

Gert took the wine glass from Molly and told her to sleep, to try, once again, to sleep. Then she blew out the candle and left the room.

It was nine o'clock when Gert went back downstairs. She expected the house to be dark. Thought everyone was exhausted. Thought everyone had gone to bed. She was startled to find Joe's father there, sitting alone, by the fire in the living room. He was smoking one of his long black cigarettes. He was sipping a glass of brandy. He chuckled when she entered the room.

"So. We're a good team, me and the boy," he said. "A good team."

"What do you mean?" Gert asked. She was wary of this man. He had too many tricks.

"We don't need the rest of you," he said. "I give you money, I tell you to get the boy out, and what do you do? You and the mother? On TV you make it look like the boy committed murder. On TV, the mother makes a spectacle of herself."

The ash on the end of his cigarette was an inch long. He made no attempt to flick it into the ashtray. He inhaled again. Still, the ash remained.

"Jimmy's going to need help," Gert said.

"You didn't see the police?" he asked. "You didn't hear it's suicide?"

"What did you do to convince them?" Gert asked.

"I told the truth," he chuckled. "That's all."

The truth? The same truth that had defeated Molly? "What truth?" she asked.

"That my son committed suicide. I knew that. I went into the house and I found him. Dead. He killed himself. But there is nothing worse. What a bum. What a coward. What a scandal. I told them I took the gun. I hid the gun. I did not want people to say my son, the judge, committed suicide. It is a disgrace I did not want. So I took the gun."

"And then you put it back?" She was sure that's what she had seen him doing today, at noon. He brought back the gun, he called the police, and he left. "When I saw you, that's when you put the gun back, isn't it?"

The old man chuckled.

"Why did you change your mind?"

"They said it was murder, the police did. They told the boy it was murder. The boy called me. He told me. Police were foolish to talk to the child like that. Foolish like a bunch of Cossacks. He told me. The boy told me."

"Did you think they suspected Jimmy?" Gert asked. "Not Molly?"

"No need to suspect anyone," the old man said. "It was suicide. I told them. Now they know."

It was odd the police believed the story. They were certainly more willing to believe him than to believe Molly. Gert remembered the old man's claim that he bought a judge's title for Joe. How much would it take, she wondered, for Cook to accept a bribe?

"Did you pay them?" Gert asked, "the police?"

"That's a foolish question," he said.

Perhaps it was. Perhaps the old man had so much power that money wasn't even an issue any more. Gert moved the fireplace screen to the side. The wood needed shifting. The fire was dying. A foolish question? She pushed at the logs with the poker, rearranging them in the grate. One broke in two, near the center where the fire had burned hottest. A few sparks tumbled out and hissed on the brick floor. The old man had always been able to get what he wanted in St. Paul. And, for the second time that day, she remembered what Joe had said about his father. How he was always in the right place at the right time. Yes. He certainly was.

"How did you know Joe was dead?" she asked.

"I saw him."

"You were there when he died?"

"No. After."

"Did Jimmy tell you? Did he call you? Is that why you went over there?"

"The boy didn't know anything."

"He didn't know you took the gun?"

"He didn't know I was in the house. No one knew."

Absolute paternal care. That's what the old man reminded Gert of, Eliot's ruined millionaire. She looked around the room. Her copy of the poems was still on the couch where she'd left it that afternoon. She picked up the book and placed it on the coffee table. "Where's Reenie?" she said and sat down.

"Fixing a bag for the boy. We're going on a trip, him and me. We're a good team."

"Now?" Gert asked. "Before the funeral?" What was Reenie thinking of?

"We're going away."

"Where?"

The old man chuckled. He shook his head. He wouldn't say.

"It's not right," Gert said. This was not what should happen. Not at all.

"Just to be sure," the old man said. "I'll take the boy away. I trusted you and his mother. But you didn't do it. So I'll take the boy myself. I know. I know how to do things. I had to do it myself once. I know when to get away."

Gert thought he knew only too well. "Why did you run away, when you were a boy? Why did you really have to leave home?"

"Trouble," the old man said. "I already told you. Trouble. My mother told me to go. I went. That's all."

"You fought with a man. What happened to him?"

The old man shook his head. Then he smiled.

"Did he die?" Gert asked.

"I don't know," he said. "How could I know? I was gone."

He was always going, it seemed. This was a man who didn't know he was part of a family, a country, a time. Didn't know he was a part of history. How could he? He swept up his past as he went along. But ever since he told that story about Russia, Gert had an idea in the back of her mind. "Who was he?" she asked. "The man on the horse?"

"A man, that's all."

There had to be more to it. "It was your father, wasn't it?" Gert asked. She had been wondering about it all afternoon. And now, the old man's determination to get his grandson out of town was making her more curious.

The old man repeated what he'd said before, "My father I never again heard about."

Gert kept thinking about her theory. Years and years ago, in Russia, he had fought with a man he said was cruel.

Probably killed him. And it probably was his own father. On horseback. A cossack. But did it matter whose father this cossack was? His mother protected him. She gave him a coat. She gave him money. She made him run. And now, it was happening all over again. Poor Jimmy. Repeating the tragedy. Reared for it. Guided, pushed, driven to it. Gert said nothing more. But it was all too apparent. It was also apparent Jimmy should not go with his grandfather. No matter what story the police accepted. No matter how many people claimed it was suicide. Suicide. That's what Gert thought at first, but not any more. Jimmy needed help. He needed care. An he wasn't going to get it from the old man. The old man would only help the boy run. Help him run, like he had run. Like they were going to run, now.

The boy came into the room with Reenie.

Reenie was smiling. "Gert," she said. "Joe's father has given Jimmy a wonderful present. A gift. So our boy can take some time and relax."

She knew about the money. Molly must have handed it over. And it didn't bother her. "Thy will be done," Gert could almost hear Reenie saying.

Joe's father put out his cigarette. He stood and walked to the door.

"Let's go," he said. "We're all ready, so let's go."

"I wish you hadn't lost your gloves, Jimmy," Reenie said. "They were very good leather gloves I bought you for your birthday. How could you lose your gloves?"

The boy looked up at his grandfather, and Gert saw the old man shake his head at him. Don't, he seemed to be saying, don't say anything.

"I can buy him five pairs of gloves," the old man said.

"Still, they must be here. He wouldn't lose those, would you Jimmy?" Reenie said. "I'll look upstairs one more time."

"So much over a single pair of gloves," Joe's father said. "Forget them. Who knows what happens to gloves? It's nothing."

But it was. It was something. Gert could feel it. She could feel fear coming from Jimmy, feel control being exerted by the old man. The gloves, don't say anything about the gloves. She could see it in the old man's eyes. She could almost hear it in the old man's breathing. And slowly, it came to her. Jimmy walking home from school, wearing his gloves. Of course, his gloves. If there had been blood on the gun, there would also be blood on the hand of the person who fired it. And there was no blood on either one of Joe's hands. In all the excitement, she'd forgotten. But the night before, she had noticed. She had looked at Joe's hands — when Martin was talking about backsplash; she remembered Joe lying there on the bed, and she remembered looking at his hands. Martin warned the other cops to check the sinks. Martin thought whoever shot Joe might have washed the blood from his hands. Of course, if it had been suicide, the blood should have been on Joe's own hands. But it wasn't. And it wasn't in the sink. And now Gert knew why. Whoever shot Joe wouldn't have to wash. Not if he were wearing gloves.

"Perhaps you left your gloves in the house," Gert said. "Your books were there last night."

Jimmy looked to his grandfather again.

"He wasn't in the house long enough to leave his gloves," the old man said.

Reenie came back. "They are not up there. They are nowhere in this house and it is cold outside. Young man, did you wear nothing on your hands when you came here last night?"

"He must have left them in my car," the old man said. "Yesterday. When I gave him a ride."

"I hope so," Reenie said. She kissed the boy on the cheek but he did not kiss her back. "It's too much for him," she said to everyone. "Way too much. He needs to get away."

But Gert didn't agree. "Jimmy," she reached toward the boy, but he moved away. "Jimmy, I don't think you should go. Does your mother want you to go?"

He did not turn around. He opened the heavy oak door for his grandfather, and followed the old man out onto the porch.

"It won't do any good. He's determined," Reenie said. "He's been through so much."

"Does Molly know?" Gert asked.

"Before we came down. She said it was a good idea, Jimmy getting away for a while, for a rest. She kissed him good-bye."

"Does she know he's going with Joe's father?" It was not making sense to Gert.

"Well yes, of course," Reenie said. "She knows it's for the best. At least for now."

"Reenie," Gert said, "somebody's got to take care of him."

"That's what we are doing, Gert. We all want Jimmy to be safe. We are taking care of him."

So that was it. Everybody did know. And Gert was the only one who believed the child should not run. She thought he should stay and face the truth. Name it. Understand it. Don't ignore it. No matter how many generations of repetition drove him. No

137

matter how much cruelty twisted him. He should not run away. He should stop. It was the only way he could go back to being the beautiful child Gert used to know. Instead, the boy was being transformed. He was growing sullen and angry.

Gert whispered to Reenie. "Just because the police say it's suicide, that doesn't mean it was."

"Gertrude," Reenie said, "I'm shocked."

Gert should have expected this from Reenie. If she was anything it was protective. Quiet. Yes. But quiet like a mother bear in the bushes, watching to be sure her cub was all right. And Molly was no different. She was a willing partner in this conspiracy. Molly was always anticipating Jimmy's abduction and now she was collaborating, protecting him by sending him away. But they weren't giving him safe conduct by letting him go. They were abandoning him. "What if he murdered his father?" Gert tried to keep her voice at a whisper. "Even if Joe did scare him into it, he can't just walk away."

"Gert," Reenie swallowed hard. "I don't believe what you're saying." She stepped back, as though the thoughts that steamed from Gert were unsavory. As though, by moving away, Reenie could avoid the vapor.

"I think you know it as well as I do," Gert said.

Jimmy's voice was loud. "I heard you, Gert," he said.

"Jimmy," Reenie said. "Gertrude didn't mean what she said. It's not what she meant to say."

"I did mean it," Gert said. "You must remember what's true. If you were hurt, say it. Go ahead. People do things because they have reasons. It's like you Mom said on TV, sometimes kids have to protect themselves. Just don't let things get mixed up. Jimmy, don't forget what's real."

Jimmy spun around and stared at Gert. His eyes were glassy. Shining, glassy.

"Jimmy, I think you should stay here." It was hard for Gert to watch the boy leave his mother like this. What would she say when she felt better ... my son, I never heard of you again? "I think if your mother thought about it, she'd want you to stay here," Gert said.

The boy shook his head and he whispered, "She's crazy."

"What?" Gert was surprised.

"My mother's the one who's crazy. And you. She made you crazy too."

The words were coming from the mouth of the child, but they belonged to his father. He wasn't a boy any longer, this infant, he was wearing the robes of the patriarch now, speaking in his tongue, becoming the very power he wished to flee. The ogre child. Was there no other way for the victim to become the victor? "My mother doesn't know anything about anything," he said it again, snickering this time. "She's just crazy."

The old man pulled the boy by the sleeve of his jacket. "Here," he said, "come here. Don't be a coward. Nobody's dead. As long as I got you, I still got a son."

"Jimmy," Gert said, "stay here."

But the boy never looked back. He tucked his arm into his grandfather's. The two of them walked shoulder to shoulder across the porch, out the door, down the stairs. That's when Gert realized they were the same size.

"Come on now," the old man kept saying. "Help me down these stairs. Come on now," he said to the boy, "Come on. Don't be such a bum. Come on."

In a few moments, they were gone.

"Don't you know why Molly let him go?" Reenie asked after the boy and the old man disappeared in the limousine. "A mother has no choice." Then Molly's mother removed herself, in silence, to her room.

Only Gert was left there, in the front hall, completely alone. Why did Molly have no choice? Of course she had a choice. Gert refused to believe otherwise. She thought about calling Cook, telling him to reopen the case as a homicide. But she knew that wouldn't work. There was a reason he believed the old man. Even if that wasn't why he dressed so well on a policeman's salary. Even if he wasn't bribed. Power. Yield to power. So simple for most people. So impossible for Gert. She walked into the pantry. There was a telephone directory on the counter. She found the listing she was looking for. She lifted the receiver, pressed seven numbers, and waited.

When the switchboard operator answered, Gert said, "Ballistics, please. Officer Martin. Is he in?"

When he came to the phone, Gert spoke carefully. She was searching for a way to help the boy. She reminded Martin about the backsplash. About how he'd worried that an assailant might have washed evidence away in the sink.

"If it was suicide, shouldn't there have been blood on Joe's hands?" Gert asked.

Martin had an answer for its absence. "I'm afraid it all ended up on your friend's coat," he said. "Most of it anyway. I'm sure that's why you didn't see any on the judge's hand. Ask the wife," he said, "although she probably doesn't remember. Terrible shock for her. Is she still in that condition? Apparently she flung herself across his body when she found him, mucked up the scene quite a bit, wiped away some things, like the blood you're talking about. Made things tough for Lieutenant Cook. Still, it's incontrovertible. It's a suicide. No doubt in my mind." Appreciated her call, he said. Lucky she phoned when she did. He was just getting ready to leave. Reports all done. Finally. Good night.

Nothing would be changed by her concern.

The old man had everything figured out, all right. By now he and Jimmy would be long gone. She knew what they were doing. They were traveling like the old man had done as a child. They were traveling by night.

She pressed the receiver into its cradle, still had her hand on it, when it rang.

"May I speak with Molly Stuart, please?" It was Sandra Gens.

Gert was not going to make the same mistake again. "No," she said. "She's asleep."

"This is Sandra Gens. I need a reaction from her. I'm writing on deadline."

"I'm afraid it's not possible," Gert said.

"Do you know if she's aware the charges have been dropped against all the parents she had arrested?"

"Yes, she's aware of that."

"Can you tell me her reaction?"

"How could I?"

"Does she know the kids have been sent home?"

"Yes."

"What did she say?"

"You'll have to talk to her tomorrow," Gert said.

"I'm sure you understand my predicament," the writer said. "A few hours ago she was a hero, now she's been publicly embarrassed. Do you have a reaction to this, this debasement?"

"She was simply trying to save the children," Gert said.

"And she was martyred along the way?"

"Martyred," Gert repeated it. It was a good word, one she had been using for Molly herself. Had she been martyred? "Yes," Gert

140

said. "Martyred."

Then Gert told the Gens woman she had no more to say. She cradled the phone one more time, went upstairs to her room, and closed the door. She began folding and packing clothes that had been unpacked only hours before. There was no more for her to do. In the morning she would leave.

CHORUS

ST. PAUL, Minn. Sticks and stones will break my bones but names will never hurt me.

Did Molly Stuart forget that rhyme? She may have. Last night she stood out in the snow and begged us all to understand what she called "The Truth."

Violence must stop, she said. No more sticks, no more stones, no more bones must be broken. And while you're at it, no more names either. She tried to convince us all that there is no difference when it comes to hurting. In fact, she said, names may hurt so bad that a child may lash out with sticks and stones — or guns and bullets — in retaliation.

Well, maybe we can accept that. But some of us could not accept how far Stuart was willing to carry her argument. If she says no more she means no more. If an adult abuses a child physically, society should not punish the child for reacting with violence. If a verbally abused child decides to kill his abuser, society should let it pass.

Stuart is nothing if not consistent. And public opinion is nothing if not swift. Stuart ended up this morning a victim of her own crusade to save the children.

And I've got a name for Molly Stuart today. The name I'm thinking about is martyr.

It's not completely my own invention. I checked it out with a close friend of Stuart, and she concurs.

But how did it happen, this fall from heroism? And why are we so sure she has indeed become a martyr for her cause?

Well, martyrs are sort of like kings and queens. One moment they have power, the next it's gone. Look at Stuart, one moment she was a warrior out on a crusade to save the children. She had power. She slew dragons. She arrested parents. She saved the innocent, attacked the wrongdoer, cleaned up the kingdom, made peace in all the land.

But suddenly last night it became apparent that she couldn't save anyone anymore. She surrendered to her own destiny. Let it be.

Because, you see, that is the calling of a martyr. A martyr can never win. A martyr's only power is the power to surrender to sacrifice. And that is what happened to Stuart last night.

Armed with a mighty truth — the only way to stop violence is to stop — she charged the dragon. Armed with a mighty truth — a child's soul is as important as his body — she charged the dragon. Armed with a mighty truth — protect the children at all costs, even if it ruins the criminal

142

justice system — she charged the dragon.

But her truth was unacceptable to the general public. They thought she was encouraging children to commit matricide and patricide. They thought she was the dragon, and we all know what happens to dragons.

The next thing she knew, the child abuse cases were taken away from her. Closed. And Stuart was forced to abandon those she meant to set free. Destiny.

She had been the knight. But last night she became the dragon. And then, almost immediately, she turned into the innocent victim, slain by her own mighty truth.

No surprise though. That's what martyrs are supposed to do. The martyr is an actor in a high class snuff film — anointed but insane — they die for the role they're assigned.

But this is where I disagree with the classical definition of martyrs. Because I know quite a few martyrs and they aren't dead at all.

They're women, most of them. Martyrdom used to come easy for women. You remember. Some martyrs demanded the right to unionize. Some demanded the right to age. Some demanded the right to have rights.

Were they sacrificed? Yes.

Are they dead and gone? No. They're pulling themselves up by their pumps. Working their way back, part-time.

Their mutilation was bloodless. As Stuart's should be.

So, Molly Stuart, if you're a real martyr, take a hint from women martyrs everywhere. Don't do anything messy like die or disappear or even allow yourself to be drummed completely out of your profession. No. Molly Stuart, if you're really a martyr — like all good female martyrs in the past — just take a low paying job as a clerk in somebody else's law firm, and start all over again.

Try again. You see, it doesn't matter how long it takes a real martyr to get to heaven.

And by the way, that's it. I have choreographed the last dance for The Chorus. Next week, I'll simply be Sandra Gens.

143

BLESSING

Gert threw the newspaper on the bed next to her duffel bag. Didn't like the way Gens talked about her — flippant — "a friend concurs." What did she mean by that? What was Molly going to think? Gert's presence hadn't helped Molly. It had only made things worse.

It had all begun with Molly's pleas for a Mass. And, like some sort of Melchisidech, Gert had hurried down from Sweetgrass to fulfill the request. But she had been foolish. She had bungled it all. She should never have let Molly talk to reporters. And she herself, she should never have talked to that columnist at all. Gert had come to offer a Mass and ended up sacrificing her friend. Molly had been held up to the world. Her beliefs scattered. Her truth immolated. Her crusade consumed.

Gert wasn't a very good priest after all.

Even so. It wasn't supposed to matter, how good she was. Shouldn't her prayers have risen to heaven no matter what? Shouldn't her prayers have risen to God?

But what if she had been offering prayers to a god who had gone bad? What then?

Gert couldn't get over the picture of Joe, blown full of rage, wreaking destruction on the creatures from whom he demanded love. So much like the god of their childhood. The scary painting on the ceiling at St. Elizabeth's. She knew she could not stay for Joe's funeral. She had not come to say a requiem for an angry god.

There was a light knock on the bedroom door. Gert opened it to find Molly standing there in the hall. In her right hand was the wash cloth Gert had given her the night before to cool her forehead. She was still wearing the maroon robe.

"Please," Molly said. "Don't go."

Gert took her by the hand. She led her into the room. She moved her bag so Molly could sit on the bed.

"I have to leave," Gert said. "I just have to go."

"I need you," Molly said. "And so does Jimmy."

"He's gone, Molly. Reenie said you knew ..." Gert looked at her friend, sitting on the bed, twisting the dry rag around her

144

fingers. "There is nothing more I can do," Gert told her.

"Yes, there is," Molly insisted. "I've been thinking. You could take me with you. We could find Jimmy and you could take us — and the others too. The children, I can't leave the children. Couldn't you take us all?"

"To Sweetgrass?" Gert asked.

"Yes. Gert, please. We'd all be safe there with you in Sweetgrass."

Gert sat down next to Molly. It was impossible to save the children. It was impossible to save Molly's own child. But she could still take the mother and run. After all, it was the mother who was being destroyed, bloodless though the newspaper said her sacrifice should be.

"Tell me about Sweetgrass," Molly said. "Tell me what Sweetgrass is like."

That was easy, Gert said, of course.

And she began with the town. The shops. The mountain roads. The log houses with stone hearths. And the people. How accepting they were. How kind. It was peaceful, Sweetgrass was. It was a good home. Then she told her about her church, how warm it was, the candles, the altar, the stained glass windows, the aroma of incense behind the great heavy doors.

"Then you'll do it?" Molly seemed serious. "You'll help me get Jimmy back? And the others? And you'll take us to Sweetgrass? You'll take us home?" There were tears in Molly's eyes, but they glistened with hope.

Gert dropped a pair of dangling silver earrings into the pocket of a lavender cotton shirt. She folded the shirt, the last of the things she needed to pack. She stooped over the duffel bag lying on the floor, tucked the shirt into a corner of the bag, and zipped it shut.

Take Molly to Sweetgrass? She knew the answer. She had known it as soon as she began to describe the town.

Sweetgrass. She could see the wooden marker by her house. Sweetgrass. She could see Henry Billingcourt talking. Sweetgrass. She could hear him telling about his people. Sweetgrass. She could hear their story.

Lead her to Sweetgrass, he would say, when you get there she can rest. Lead her to Sweetgrass, he would say, when you get there, she'll be safe.

Gert took Molly by the hand. "Maybe," she said and she

145

walked with her friend down the stairs, around the bend that led to the kitchen. Maybe. She had even said the word to herself.

But she knew as she made strong black coffee. She knew as she poured heavy cream into blue porcelain cups. She knew as she heard Henry Billingcourt's words in her mind. "Take her to Sweetgrass ..." his voice was saying. "Take her to Sweetgrass ... She'll be safe."

But Gert knew there was no need, no need at all. The Sweetgrass borderline had been moved again, just like years ago when Chief Joseph was fooled into thinking he and his people had found safety in Canada. No, Molly didn't have to run away to find a place where the boundary lines were constantly being erased. She didn't have to go anywhere to find Sweetgrass — she was already there.

Sweetgrass was edited in Microsoft Word 2.0 for Windows 3.1
and typeset on a LaserMaster LM1000 Plain-Paper Typesetter at
Lone Oak Press